THE SPIRITS OF
PULHAMS MILL

All rights reserved.

No part of this book may be reproduced or transmitted in any form or by any means, electronic or mechanical, including photocopying, recording, or by any information storage and retrieval system without the written permission of the author, except where permitted by law. This is a work of fiction. The characters, incidents and dialogue are drawn from the author's imagination and are not to be construed as real. Any resemblance to actual events or persons, living or dead, is entirely coincidental.

Published in Great Britain 2023
Copyright © 2023 Powers Ian Mawby
First edition

The drawings are illustrated by Pauline Clements.
Formatting and Book Design by FlintlockCovers.com.

THE SPIRITS OF PULHAMS MILL

THE AUCTION ROOM

POWERS IAN MAWBY

*Dedicated to Pauline, my wife,
who patiently collaborated in the design
and drew the original pen and ink illustration.*

Contents

Prologue	1
1. The Auction	2
2. Edmund the Younger's Story	9
3. Robert Miller's Story	14
4. Peter Gadd's Story	20
5. Anna Miller's Story	26
6. Francis Westcott's Story	47
7. Jerry Winzor's Story– Part 1	95
8. Jerry Winzor's Story – Part 2	114
9. Jerry's Winzor's Story – Part 3	184
10. William Parker's Story	196
11. Jerry Winzor's Story – Part 4	217
12. Francis Pestone's Story	227
13. Fran and Peter's Story	233
14. The Second Auction	252
Epilogue	262

Prologue

I will relate to you the strange story of this ancient Mill on the River Pulham where spirits rule and take control of who should be allowed to buy it.

Fran and Peter bought Pulhams Mill, a beautiful romantic ruin mentioned in the (1086) Domesday Book, in 1978. They saved it from falling down and restored it to its former glory. Then, as a life-changing project they ran it as a tea room and craft centre. But they were forced by the banks to put it on the market. During the next four years, it had nearly sold several times, but each time, at the last moment, the buyers had dropped out for no apparent reason.

A friend, who also happens to be a shaman, dowsed the Mill and reported that there were several spirits inhabiting it.

So, Peter and Fran decided to auction their beautiful ancient home and business.

But still the spirits resisted all attempts to sell it.

Green Oak Barn

CHAPTER 1

The Auction

PULHAMS MILL GREEN OAK
BARN, 29 OCTOBER 2020

The room filled up! Lillie was at the reception desk, welcoming and directing the people to their seats. Not all 65 seats were taken although there were people already standing at the back!

It was a little strange as there were several seats in the middle of the first and second rows which had not been taken; it felt as if they had been reserved. But still, there was apparently nothing to hinder people from sitting in those seats.

As the time to start the auction got closer, the clamour of anticipation and the volume of conversations rose!

Paul, the auctioneer, left it until it reached its peak to get the adrenaline rising and to encourage interest!

'Good day, ladies and gentlemen!' He tapped the gavel to gain attention. 'My name is Paul Borrows and I will be your auctioneer for today's proceedings. Today we have several properties to sell at auction. Those details should have been placed on your seat before you sat down. If not, you may pick them up from Lillie at the desk at the door. The details are also online. If you don't have a copy, Lillie will bring you one. Before we start, could some of you standing at the back possibly move into the five empty seats at the front here?'

Nobody seemed to want to move.

Paul noticed that the seats that were vacant did not have property details on them. He thought that Lillie must have just missed them. But it was strange because he was almost certain that she had put them there earlier. So, he shrugged to himself. 'Anyway!' He had better just proceed.

'The first property is Pulhams Mill. This is an ancient property, mentioned in the Domesday Book. This was Norman's account of the ownership of their annexed land:

After the defeat of Harold at Hastings, the Mill was possessed by Harold's mother, Gytha. It has a great history and should be bought by a person who would take the property to the next level and who would put the same love and care that the present owners have taken into renovating it and protecting it from the inappropriate renovation. The property is not listed but needs to survive without significant change for another thousand years.

'We are to auction the property as one of two lots. The first lot is the whole of the site at a guide price of £950,000. This comprises both the main house; the ground floor tea rooms, 3-bedroom flat above and an acre field on the north side of the lane, plus the 3-bedroom stone cottage rental/ holiday let on the south side of the road adjacent to the 15 by 6 metre two-storey Green Oak Barn that we are holding the auction in. This building comprises a furniture workshop on the ground floor and a teaching and music venue here on the first floor.

'If lot 1 is passed in as unsold, then the part of the property which is on the north side of the lane will be sold as lot 2. This comprises the main house, stone barn, and an-acre field with a guide price of £415,000. As can be seen from the details, the main house is a substantial stone building with a slate roof. On the ground floor is a tea room/restaurant that could seat 20/30 covers, a three-bedroom owner's flat on the first floor, an adjacent stone barn shop and customer parking for seven cars and a one-acre field lies behind and above the Mill.

'Lot 1! Can I have offers in excess of £950,000 for the whole?"

Paul then experienced a very strange feeling that there was a presence emanating from the empty seats in the front and second row of the room. It felt like a barrier between him and the audience. He couldn't see anything, but it seemed that more than one entity was preventing people from putting in a bid. He had never experienced anything like this in a saleroom in 20 years. His laptop lost signal! The lights dimmed, and silence fell in the room!

Then, people started to walk out very quietly. It was as if the auction was over! He tried to pull the whole thing back together. But the words that he was almost shouting just seemed to bounce back!

'Pulhams Mill Tea Rooms.'

Paul couldn't work it out.! There was nothing in his power that he could do about it! He lost all recognition of time. It seemed as if one of the spirits from the empty seats was guiding him out of Green Oak Barn and into the past!

Paul followed cautiously; the road didn't appear to be made up. It was just a sea of mud and stone. The bridge seemed to have disappeared. There was a splash instead. The uneven lane had cartwheel-width tracks and hoof marks as if the cavalry had just passed through.

There was no sign of his new BMW, which he had parked about two and a half hours ago or of the audience of 60 people that had so recently been in the barn and their cars were all gone! What on earth was going on! It was not at all earthly and Paul started to panic as he was just swept away into what seemed to be another century. Another world!

And then suddenly and strangely, as he walked back into the Mill, he had no mud on his shoes. He had just dropped back into the now. The tea room was the same as he had photographed last month, and the tables were set out in the same way they had been an hour and a half ago!

Around the big table, there was a group of very strangely dressed figures and a dog with the name Millie on a brass tag that seemed to be flashing. He could plainly see five spirits, but there seemed to be one or maybe two other ghost-like figures floating around them. They were each dressed in styles of clothing from different periods in history. They were arguing violently about something. He could hardly understand what they were arguing about. It seemed to be a mixture of English and something akin to French! Every now and again, Millie the dog, a mixed collie-Labrador, would bark as if she was putting in her own opinion.

Paul stood there in amazement at this scene!

There was a barrier between him and the group around the table. He tried to approach the table, but he could only get to within three feet of the bickering group. He tried to put a word in, just to ask what was going on.

The character who seemed to be the leader replied to Paul's enquiry with a look that would have withered a lesser person! It was obvious that they could hear Paul. But there was a force that held him back from any physical contact. The argument was made worse as the characters didn't seem to understand each other. But it seemed to be about who was a suitable person to buy the Mill. Then, as if running a film, a procession of ghost-like people, whom he thought he recognised from the auction, passed by the table within the space that was barred to Paul. They didn't seem real. He put his hand out to touch them, to feel if they were there or not. There was a distinct chill as his hand got close to an inviolable barrier.

One of the group around the table was questioning the first prospective buyer. What did he intend to use the Mill for after the purchase? Paul could not hear what the reply was as the volume of the argument surged to a crescendo of disapproval which included a growling bark from the dog! The interviewing continued as each of the prospective buyers was questioned in turn by each of the quorum. And after each of the interviewees was questioned, there was an uproar of disapproval, then eerie silence. The interviews were over, broken by another chorus of disapproval by all the prospective buyers.

It appeared that the spirits had come to the decision that none of the prospective buyers should be allowed to purchase what they considered to be their property. Each of the five spirits around the table (as spirits they must be) took the centre of vision, and the others, although still there, faded into the background.

Each of them told their stories and then gave an account of how they had become Spirits of the Mill.

Brompton Manor, Gytha's residence, AD 1069

CHAPTER 2

Edmund the Younger's Story

First up was Edmund the Elder, who told the story of and for, his son who fought against 'William the Bastard' with Harold's army at Hastings. He died of his wounds at the Mill having returned from the battle.

Edmund the Elder, the miller from the mill on the Pulham River, was waiting to see Gytha Thorkelsdóttir, Harold Godwinson's mother. She was very busy as her servants packed what was left of her chattels so she could flee from William.

Edmund the Elder had known Gytha for many years as a young lass, at the time of her son, Harold Godwinson's, birth. He was concerned about the possession of Gytha's lands at Brompton. These lands had been hers and in the Godwinson family's lordship for nearly 200 years. This would mean that Edmund might lose his livelihood and his home of 30 years, and he and his children would be left destitute. His eldest son, also called Edmund, had fought and been badly injured at the Battle of Hastings. He would be marked as an enemy of William. However, Edmund the Elder didn't want to move his son as he could be very near to death. If the family had to flee with Gytha, Edmund's wife would not be happy as it would mean that her eldest son would be left to die alone at the Mill.

William's henchmen were going from village to village taking a reckoning to make sure that villagers had accounted correctly for the land and properties that had been taken from Harold at the Battle of Hastings. This reckoning and record would become known as the *Domesday Book* and is still in existence in the present day.

William had issued a decree that Gytha should not be harmed, but those orders had been written in Norman French, and in any case, most of the men couldn't read or write, so the decree would have been passed by word of mouth. They could end up like whispers being passed from one to the next, and inevitably they would get changed.

A lot of the henchmen were very poor deserters from Harold's army; some were Picts or Scots. Others would join any army that would allow them to survive in the era of death, anarchy and destruction that followed the defeat of Harold.

Although Edmund was only a miller, he was in a position of trust as he had saved Gytha the Younger's (Harold's wife) life when she was only 12.

Gytha was preparing to leave. She was going to flee to Flanders and needed to leave soon, but she could not organise a big enough boat to make the crossing. She had asked Edmund and his family to travel with her. He said he couldn't leave his son to die alone, but stated his other son Edgar and his daughters, Edith and Salany, would be glad to accompany her. He would stay at the Mill with his son Edmund the Younger.

So Gytha asked Edmund to organise a small boat to take her and a few trusted supporters to Steep Holm, a small island in the channel off Dunster. She had to avoid contact with the emissaries of William as his relation, William I de Moyon, had taken the hill fort at Dunster, and there was a constant watch to catch those who were fleeing after he had annexed the landing places.

Dunster hill fort

Edmund borrowed a horse from Gytha and made haste to contact his cousin's son, Magnus, who was a fisherman out of Watchet. He trusted him as he had always been close to his daughter, Edith. Magnus was enamoured with Edith, but being a first cousin, there was opposition to them marrying!

When he arrived, he found Magnus having an argument with his father, Reginald, who thought it was too risky to ferry people fleeing from William's henchmen. As Watchet was the obvious port to use, Edmund agreed to help, and so they decided that the best place to set off from would be the small inlet of Gray Rock. It was difficult to get to but was also out of sight of Dunster. Edmund gave Magnus some silver penny coins that Gytha had given him to distribute to his trusted helpers. So, Gytha's escape was organised and Edmund the Elder returned to Brompton to give the news to Gytha. He arrived back to hear that his son, Edmund, was very near to death, so he decided to stay at the Mill and bury his son there, and take his chances with the henchmen, in the hope that his family could return when they moved on.

Before leaving her lands at Brompton, Gytha went to the Mill to pay her respects to Edmund the Younger, who had been a loyal supporter and friend to her son Harold.

Edmund the Elder buried his son on a hill behind the Mill without ceremony, apart from prayers, from Joseph, the local priest. He placed a large rock of shining quartz as his headstone *(which to this day on the hill is known as: 'Shining Stone')*.

CHAPTER 3

Robert Miller's Story

THE MILL ON THE RIVER
PULHAM, 1490

William de Say founded Barlynch Priory in 1154. He also had possession of the Mill on the Pulham River that supplied flour and grain to the priory and the village.

In 1478 William Hampney became the prior of Barlynch (St Nicholas) and was granted a charter for two annual fairs (which, very unusually, would last over many millennia).

Since 1070 the Mill had been operated by the same family of millers. The present miller, Reginald, was a descendant of Magnus Miller and a cousin of Edmund, who was respected as a constant. He had seen several priors come and go. The Mill had become an important part of the village and the Droving Road.

Reginald's second son, Robert, was very aware of the importance of the Mill and was keen to develop it as a source of income while he was young and able. But Robert liked to gamble. He looked forward to the drovers coming and stopping over as they all gambled. They were able to use the wide unfenced edges of the droving track to graze their flocks and stay overnight before the fairs at Bury and Brompton.

William Hampney, the prior of Barlynch (or St Nicholas), had possession of the Mill as part of the Williton Hundreds. William was also a gambler, but this was a kept secret. If Alice Chester of Bristol got wind of it, he would lose his stipend.

He would only come to the Mill in the dead of night. Robert found a secluded part of the Mill, the back kitchen, where there was an open fire lit and where the light couldn't be seen by the drovers' camp just up the hill.

William arrived on foot on a very wet night; he had to cross the ford over the Pulham River. When he arrived, he was not over hasty to sit at the gaming pit as he was very wet. Robert's mother, Gahan, ministered to him, helping him off with his very wet boots and coat. William expected to be treated with respect, so she poked the fire and fussed around him; he was their lord, after all. He was given some mead and freshly baked bread to enjoy in front of the fire and when he had finished, he left the clothes steaming and stinking close to the roaring fire. Gahan put another log on the fire.

Just then two trusted elders from the village, who were keen gamblers, arrived to join the game of Chance, which was played with dice. But William said that he wanted to play a new game that had recently come from Italy and had become very popular in France. Robert wasn't keen on this as he knew how to cheat on Chance, but William told Robert to organise a table saying, 'This is a card game.'

After a lot of moving and disturbance, with the table arranged and the oil lamps and candles lit, they settled down to play.

William chose to be the banker (as in Baccarat the banker is always at an advantage). The first few hands were for small amounts of farthings and half pennies and went in William's favour as he knew the game. (He had played with his relations in Paris the previous year and had lost heavily! He thought that this was a way to regain his swagger.) He hadn't reckoned on Robert being a very clever gambler.

Robert very quickly mastered Nines. He let William win for several rounds as the stakes got bigger. The villagers, Jon and Percy, dropped out as the stakes were getting too high for them. Robert slowly started moving in for the kill! It was his turn to be the banker. William could see that his plan wasn't working, but as he had lost a considerable amount of silver pennies and gold coins, he was determined to win his money back. In the last round, he felt that he was certain to win! He wagered a legal note for ownership of the Mill against the pot of silver and gold coins. Robert won the round, and the Mill was his! And he hadn't even needed to cheat. His luck was in! But there was an argument, and William accused him of cheating. Robert had the legal note, demanding, 'How *could* I have cheated? This is the first time I have played Nines. It was beginner's luck!

William tried to snatch back the note. Robert had expected that. He knew that William would be a bad loser! He shouldn't have been there secretly gambling in the first place. The Mill was not his personal property to lose, so he couldn't make too much of a scene. So, William put on his very hot boots that had been so near the fire. (He was lucky that they hadn't burst into flames.) Then he put on his steaming coat and stomped out. Cursing and threatening Robert and Reginald with the wrath of God, he stomped out into the pouring rain to walk through the ford and back three miles to St Nicholas Priory (Barlynch).

Robert was very pleased about winning the Mill. But his father, Reginald, who was a man of God, was worried as he felt that winning it from the prior would bring family problems. He did not approve of gambling, but he was convinced by his first son, Reginald the Younger, that it was a good thing and it meant that the future of the family at Pulhams Mill was secured. Reginald tried, rather half-heartedly, to discourage Robert from gambling. He didn't want to lose the Mill. So, he arranged the next day to play a game of dice with a bunch of drovers who had arrived from the levels for the fair.

(II)
ROBERT WAS ON A ROLL!

Robert was ready for them before sundown. It was spring and still a little chilly on the hills. So they played in a shed in the field above the Mill to be out of the way of Robert's father, who was liable to come and break up the game. Robert had worked out that in the half-light, as the sun went down, he could get away with cheating; he could conceal the loaded die, so he knew when to bet!

Robert didn't recognise the bearded drover who had joined the game. Robert had won quite a lot from a man called Grange the previous June, but Buster Grange was not going to lose anymore! Then Robert cast the weighted die. Grange knew that the die was loaded and challenged Robert for cheating. Robert denied it, but there was uproar!

Grange knocked Robert to the floor and took the loaded die, and pressed the sharp corners of it into Robert's palm. This marked him as a cheat, so he couldn't play Chance anymore. He was much deflated and left the game, and this seemed to be the end of his gambling. He tried to scrub out the mark with a rusty iron brush. It just made it worse! The next day the wound was very bad, and Gahan, his mother, bathed it and bandaged it, but still, it didn't heal. It was becoming very swollen and red, going from his hand right up his arm. It was very painful, so he washed it again. He didn't realise that the water he washed it in had been tainted by the drover's piss. Ironically this was to be his downfall, and his whole body was poisoned. This left Reginald the Younger with his mother, Gahan, to run the Mill

He died about a week later and was buried very close to Edmund the younger at Shinning Stone.

Barlynch Priory lookout

CHAPTER 4
Peter Gadd's Story

DECEMBER 1535

The Mill was still in the ownership of the Miller family after Robert's death. His father had always favoured Robert, his second son. Reginald the Elder went into mourning.

The eldest son was not very happy as he felt that he had been overlooked. He should have been the most important progeny of the family. His mother, Gahan, tried to keep the peace, and his sister, who had a special place in her heart for her elder brother, tried very hard to mend the breach in this previously very close family. The gap only seemed to grow as her father was inconsolable. He then became ill and died of a broken heart.

Although Robert had been a tearaway, he had been full of life and vigour! Reginald the Elder had wanted him to be the person to carry on running the Mill (even though, at the time, he hadn't been happy about him winning the Mill from the prior.) Until Robert won the Mill, the Millers could only make bread using the leftover flour to sell to the villages. This was a very meagre living.

But after Robert won the title from Prior William, it had increased the family's income and standing in the village and surrounding area. Gahan's bread had become famous. People from as far away as Williton, Watchet, and even Taunton, would come to buy her bread. The fame of her bread spread via the drovers, who mostly came from the levels to bring their sheep to the fairs in Brompton and Bury. Gahan also took several baskets of bread to the fairs to sell.

Previously, the priory would have wanted a very large chunk of the pennies that the miller's wife had made at the fairs, and as it was, they still had to pay a tithe to sell at a fair, but it was a lot less than before!

Prior William de Hampney tried to contest the title, but Reginald the younger resisted these attempts to bully the family. Gahan knew Alice Chester from Bristol, who had made substantial donations to the priory. So William was warned off. If Alice had got to know that William had been gambling and lost the title to the Mill, he would have lost his position.

But now there were rumblings as it seemed very likely that Barlynch would be dissolved, as this was happening all over England. The monks foolishly believed that because the priory was very isolated and did not seem to be very important, they would be left alone. They should have realised that Henry's need for money and his need to root out any connections with the Catholic Pope was insatiable! The canons realised almost too late.

In 1536 they had to do something to protect themselves, an early warning of the approach of Henry's soldiers. William decided to build a watch tower at the top of Bury Hill with a passage tunnelling under the earth down to St Nicholas (Barlynch). This took about three months to build, and the Brompton villagers and the miners from Washford were expected to work to save the religious centre. They were rewarded with bread and grain from the mill.

The prior and monks felt that they could escape by keeping a regular watch from the tower, so they could see Henry's soldiers coming from the Exeter direction. Prior William de Hampney made a serious miscalculation. The soldiers came from two directions. A group came from Taunton and passed the Mill on the River Pulham. They found the tower and frightened Peter Gadd, the watchman, who ran off, but he fell and broke his leg. One of the soldiers caught up with him. Peter had a knife and managed to stab the soldier and cut him badly. This gave Peter time to limp away, dragging one leg. He managed to hide and put a splint on his leg. He very slowly made his way across the country via Red Cross, about 2 miles, to Brompton.

He decided the best thing to do was to hole up in the church. He planned to barricade the iron-clad oak door, but luck was not with him! He opened the door and found ten of Henry's soldiers camping at the entrance. He turned to hobble away, but a brute of a sergeant realised Peter was a fugitive and pursued him down the steep path. Peter fell heavily against a headstone and stunned himself for a short time. Peter managed to trip the soldier as he swiped at him with his sword and was badly cut. The sergeant fell and hit his head on a gravestone, giving Peter time to make his escape as the other nine soldiers were too drunk to follow.

He hobbled down the track and found a hiding place in a bush where he tried to stem the flow of blood with his torn shirt. He knew that he needed to find a place to hide and recover. He had to cross fields as there were soldiers all over the tracks! So he decided to walk down the leat to the mill, as that way he would not leave a trail of blood for the soldiers to follow.

Slowly he made his way through the holding ponds to the millpond. He was losing a great deal of blood, but he knew he would have sanctuary in the Mill. He sat on the wall at the edge of the millpond to rest. Gahan, the miller's wife, saw him come and helped him into a shed where she laid him on a sack full of straw and dressed his wounds. Peter was losing a lot of blood and was starting to feel very cold, so Gahan half carried him into the mill and lay him near the bread oven.

(II)
AT THE TOWER AT THE TOP OF BURY HILL

Henry's soldiers filled in the exit from the passageway into the tower. The monks thought they could escape up the passageway, but they didn't realise that it had been blocked!

A group of soldiers who had come up the Exe Valley caught the monks by surprise as they tried to escape up the passageway along with some of their servants and guards! The soldiers killed the guards and imprisoned ten canons, their cook, and their servants.

(III)
BACK AT THE MILL

Meanwhile, back at the Mill, Peter was in a very bad way, and Gahan had called Reginald to see if he could help. Reginald ran into the village to find Cedricson, the local herbalist. The herbalist was tending his garden, but he could see that Reginald was very distressed. He picked up a few things that he thought might help and accompanied Reginald back to the Mill.

When he saw Peter, he realised that he had lost a lot of blood and had no way to replace the loss. He tried a trick he had picked up on battlefields, which sometimes worked. He inserted fresh milk into a vein to replace the lost blood! It seemed to help for a few hours, but Peter was fading fast, and there didn't seem to be much hope.

Having done their worst at the Bury Hill tower, a raggedy mob of Henry's soldiers were making their way back towards Taunton past the Mill. A couple of them broke away and banged on the door, demanding bread. Reginald opened the door, as he knew that if he didn't, they would have it down.

As he opened it, they barged their way in. Reginald made haste to the oak bread box. He picked out the previous day's loaves that were still fresh and tried to herd the soldiers away from the oven where Peter lay.

An oafish soldier saw Peter and realised that he was the fellow who had opened the door of the church and run off. He saw that Peter was not long for this world! He drew his sword and said, 'I'll put him out of his misery.'

Gahan barred his way and tried to stop him, but the soldier was too big and strong, and pushed her out of the way and succeeded in fatally slashing Peter across his throat.

Peter Gadd passed over.

CHAPTER 5

Anna Miller's Story

BROMPTON, APRIL 1606

The miller, Edgar's wife, Eleanor, had five children: three daughters, Anna, Bronwyn, and Millie, and two sons, Gerald, and Joseph, the fifth child who had died at birth.

After Edgar the miller passed away, the third child and only son Geral carried on the family tradition of milling after his father. The eldest daughters were matched very quickly as they were both very handsome women. Millie was still young, but she was developing into a buxom beauty, too. Anna, the eldest, was matched with the son of the vicar and destined to soon become the incumbent of St Decuman's Church in Watchet and chaplain of Wyndham Chapel on the Wyndham family estate that had ownership of large tracts of land and houses at Williton.

John Wyndham was the third son of the family and had been a bit of a problem as a young man, so the family were glad to have him settled with a local girl. As happened, John had met Anna when he was visiting Brompton market to buy 'Grandmother Gahan's' bread. Anna's sisters, Bronwyn and Millie, were now baking, carrying on the tradition that their grandmother and mother had taught them.

Pulhams Mill had become very renowned for Gahan's bread. This brought a lot of people to the village, and the Mill, as well as to the markets, which were still being held in Brompton and Bury.

Anna was feted locally as the village beauty. She had black hair and light skin, not fat, but curvy, with green eyes. She was outgoing and loved to take the bread to the markets. This was very good for sales as there always seemed to be a queue of young men wanting to buy bread for their families.

On the occasions when Bronwyn and Millie went to market, the sales went down. It was sad as Bronwyn was a good looker as well. She didn't really care for being admired as she was shy and loved to sing and play the instrument that her father had bought her, a mandóra lute. When she wasn't kneading dough for the bread, she spent time playing in an ensemble in St Mary's church, but she was at home a lot and helped her mother.

Anna was spotted by John Wyndham one day at the market, and he started courting her. At first, Anna played it very cool as she felt that he would take advantage of his position as a son of the Wyndhams, and she was only a miller's daughter. He was to be a vicar and appeared to be an honourable man. She told her brother about it, and he was in favour of the match as it would consolidate the dynasty of the family. But as he was now head of the family, he wanted a word with John first. John beat him to it, as he was very keen to show that he was serious about the relationship. He came to see Gerald and told him that he was smitten with his sister and wanted to take Anna to meet his family! For her part, Anna was really pleased to have a good-looking man, and the son of the Wyndhams with prospects, to take her to the coast where life was more exciting. At the age of 17, she would be expected to marry soon. The alternatives were to marry a yeoman farmer, James Dunn, whom she really liked, but the die was cast. Gerald, her brother, took Anna to meet the Wyndham family.

John and Anna were engaged to be married in the spring.

Up in the hills, people felt they were a million miles away from the troubles of the coast. There was a lot of excitement in the parish because the decision was made by the Wyndham family that the wedding would be in St Mary's in Brompton. Spring was just around the corner, and the weather was looking to be set fine for a late April wedding.

The preparations started in the Miller household. Bronwyn was really pleased as she would be Anna's maid of honour and could dress up and play her lute at the wedding breakfast. Anna was excited but at the same time, sad. It had been her father's wish that he would live to see his beautiful daughter married into the top family. Eleanor, her mother, was very pleased, but her health was not good. However, she was keeping it together. Bronwyn and Millie were very busy making a dress for Anna's big day.

The family were all making preparations for the breakfast and decorating the church. They were going to have the breakfast in the great hall of Brompton Manor, and the stone masons were working to secure the building, as Gytha's Manor had been derelict for many years.

Unfortunately, the building was very unstable, and one of the villagers, Harold by name, was working on the roof, and there was a rumbling and crumbling that seemed to be issuing from an underground movement. The walls seemed to shake. The village helpers and the stonemasons ran out of the building as stones and slates fell in all directions! Harold jumped off the roof on to cart of hay that was parked close to the wall. He was very lucky! As he jumped down from the cart, a large part of the roof, slates and oak beams, descended as one onto the cart and crushed it, missing him by inches while he ran away from the disaster.

So that was it; the breakfast couldn't be held in the old manor.

The villagers were very disappointed, but the Wyndham family decided that the breakfast should now be held at Orchard Wyndham. The problem was that it would take quite a long time to get from the church to the Great Hall at Orchard Wyndham in Williton. The weather seemed to be set fine. The Miller family and the village guests were happy as it would mean that a lot of the food would be supplied by the Wyndhams. Eleanor, the bride's mother, insisted that she should do the cake, decorate the tables, and a lot of the food preparation for the breakfast.

(II)
ST MARY'S CHURCH, BROMPTON
22 APRIL 1606. THE BIG DAY ARRIVED

For over a week beforehand, the wives of the village worked to decorate St Mary's. As spring burgeoned, the church was awash with flowers. The overwhelming colour was yellow, the colour of broom, which was very apt, as the name of the village, Brompton, was derived from brōm, meaning broom, and tūn, meaning farm or settlement.

The whole village turned out in their finest. The church was filled to overflowing. Even the defrocked Catholic priest, Fingal, managed to find a new hat to doff to the bride. He caused a bit of a scene just before the bride arrived by riding up the aisle of the church on his donkey, and the inevitable happened, but the mess was cleared up very quickly.

John Wyndham was not best pleased. It happened in front of his family and the celebrant, James, the suffragan Bishop of Taunton. This was a great honour for the Wyndhams as he would only undertake weddings for special occasions. They were close friends, and Bishop James had christened John and encouraged him to join the church. He had to travel a fair distance and would attend the breakfast at Wyndham Orchard. He was never one to miss a good feast and to wish his prodigy well in his marriage and investiture as the Vicar of St Decumans.

Bessie Halse was to play the virginal but had a panic attack that morning and was being ministered to by Bronwyn. Bessie was very overweight and had become very excited about the wedding. Bronwyn managed to get her seated on the stool. Once Bessie was there, she was calm and able to play the wedding tunes on the new instrument that had been installed by the Wyndham family for the occasion. Bessie had been practising for the last month but was very uncertain. So, Bronwyn was standing by with her lute.

Bronwyn was Anna's maid of honour and Millie, her bridesmaid, so they had to rush to meet Anna. They ran down the lane towards the Mill. When they reached it, Anna was in tears outside. Normally, the prospective groom should have walked up to the church with the bride, but John Wyndham had broken with tradition and waited in the church for Anna.

Bronwyn decided that the best thing to do was to walk with Anna themselves. They sent Geffrey, one of the boys who worked in the Mill, to tell Gerald what was happening. They set off, accompanied by the village girls dressed in spring dresses with daisy chain crowns, laughing, dancing, running ahead, and teasing, making comments and suggestive jokes about the wedding night. It wasn't raining, but there was a big black cloud looming over the church, which felt like a bad omen. But just as they arrived at the wicket gate, the sun came out and lit up the festive scene. The gate was festooned and tied closed with broom-coloured ribbons by the village girls. Anna had to throw coins for them so they would let her in, and then it was up the path to the church door.

Anna arrived, but John wasn't there either. Anna's mother, Eleanor, and brother Gerald were waiting at the church door to give Anna away. The whole congregation was waiting with bated breath.

Bessie was signalled that all was ready! She started to play haltingly and then got into full swing. Eleanor, preceding her daughter proudly, walked down the aisle to her seat in the front row. Anna and her brother, arm in arm, processed up the aisle. The sun was streaming through the stained glass windows, lighting up Anna in her gown of spring green and broom yellow, which Bronwyn had designed and then made with the help of her sister. Bronwyn and Millie were there, holding their flowers and making certain that Anna didn't trip on her skirts.

There was an intake of breath …!

The congregation turned to see the dark-haired beauty in her broom-coloured dress with a posy of red and blue spring flowers glide towards the altar where John Wyndham was waiting for his future wife.

John and Anna Wyndham walked up the aisle to the west door and out into the sunlight of a beautiful spring day to the ringing of the bells and cheers from the assembled villagers. The sun had blessed the union.

The Wyndhams, Bishop James, the Miller family and selected guests from St Mary's made their way on various forms of transport down to the coast to Wyndham Orchard for the wedding feast. This took more than an hour for the bride and groom in the Wyndham's lightweight two-horse carriage. John's mother, father, and sister rode alongside the carriage. Bishop James rode his fine horse and pushed it hard to get there first. Eleanor and Gerald followed on the best hay wain with two cart horses. The invited villagers found any farm cart they could. But they would have missed most of the festivities.

The bride and groom arrived and then went into an anteroom to recover from the trip and await the arrival of their guests.

(III)
THE GREAT HALL ORCHARD, WYNDHAM

The Hall was decorated with garlands and paper chains, and spring flowers of yellow and red hung over the family portraits.

An archway of green spring beech leaves with daisies, daffodils and bluebells woven in between the leaves hung over the seats at the head of the top table for the bride and groom. On the table was a tart of shortbread in the shape of a badge with an egg custard jelly decorated with the Wyndham's coat of arms. The main table was piled high with fruits, and ten plates were overflowing with sweet piccalilli, sweetmeats, and jellies. A hog's head had been roasted, and there were also 12 plates of roast poultry, pheasants, smoked fish, jellied eels, vegetable potage, dried fruits, dates from north Africa, exotic dishes from the New World and French wines. The 2-foot-high layered cake in the shape of a watermill, baked by Eleanor, stood in pride of place. The tables were arranged in a T shape, with the top table reserved for the bride and groom, their families and, of course, Bishop James.

Bronwyn and Millie had left St Mary's early and ridden on borrowed horses down to Wyndham Orchard to set up their musical instruments in the gallery above the feast in the Great Hall.

The guests were happily arguing as to who should sit where while the servants were trying to direct them to their appointed seats. A great noise of laughing and wonder was echoing in the ceiling.

Someone struck an unseen gong. Silence! The musicians struck up a wedding tune as Anna and John processed into the Great Hall. It was as if the king and queen had arrived!

They took their seats at the top table with Eleanor and Gerald on the left and John and Greta Wyndham and Bishop James on the right. Toasts were made, and the feasting began, continuing till sundown. The Miller family and Bishop James stayed overnight. The villagers had to make their drunken way back.

A month later, John was invested as the Vicar of St Decuman's in Watchet, and the couple settled into the everyday of church life.

(IV)
WATCHET, 30 JANUARY 1607

Anna had fallen pregnant very soon after they married and was still happily doing the duties of a vicar's wife. John tried to convince her that she should take it easy as she was about to produce! Anna wouldn't hear of it! She was going to do her duties until the due date.

She was visiting the parishioners at about 8.30 in the morning and was nearing the fisherman's cottages at Doniford Bay, near the coast when there was a rumbling under their feet and a great feeling of insecurity.

The buildings seemed to shake a little. This was very unusual.

It didn't last for long.

The fishermen's wives came out of their cottages to find out what was going on. Then there was an eerie quiet, which worried the people. They felt that this was a warning from God! (They were correct). Some started up the hill to St Decumans for security, and as a place that God would protect.

So it was that just after 9 a.m., Anna was helping the elderly out of the cottages and encouraging them to make their way up the hill. The light seemed to fade as the sun was blocked out. It was as if a great monster was breathing in and sucking, pulling the air back to the ocean.

Then a great wall of water, 30 feet high, raged towards the cottages. Anna ran to escape, but it was upon her in an instant. She was washed against a wooden fence which gave way, and the wave seemed to crash down and wash her through the open door of a substantial stone cottage. She managed to hang on to the staircase and pull herself out of the torrent! The staircase was crushed by the flood and broke up, but Anna managed to pull herself up to the next floor, which was concertinaed and breaking up as she found sanctuary behind the strongest part of the building. The chimney, which had steep stones, allowed Anna to climb onto what was left of the roof. All around her was a raging, deep, black sea. She could see the wave moving relentlessly up the river valley, taking with it houses, people, cattle, sheep, fishing boats and everything that couldn't withstand the strength of this incredible brown and black monster that was consuming anything in its way.

Anna was in trouble as her waters had broken, and she was about to give birth, stranded in a raging lake. She noticed a man clambering up onto the roof. It was John, her husband.

(V)
ST DECUMANS

John had watched the wave from the church on the hill and was helping all the people who had come up from Watchet. A fisherman's wife he knew as Jessie said she thought Anna had been washed away or she might have been washed into her cottage, which was still standing! The cottage was a little higher than the others. Unusually, it was a narrow three-storey building and had been protected from the monster wave by the fish market building, which had also stood firm.

John immediately ran down the path from the church to the water's edge. As luck would have it, there was a dinghy that had been washed up. He found a plank of wood to use as an oar to paddle his way against the tide. The dinghy was washed backwards towards the cottage. He could see a woman on the roof!

He was being washed into an eddy to one side of the cottage, and the dinghy was being spun like an autumn leaf in it. John managed to steer the boat towards the door and catch onto the frame. He pulled the dinghy in and jammed it in the doorway. How to get onto the roof?

He heard Anna shouting above the tumult of crashing and cracking buildings. The water in the cottage was calm, eddying and pouring out of the windows, but he managed to swim a few strokes to what was left of the stairs and clamber up to the chimney and then up to the roof. It seemed stable, and he found Anna panicking, trying to hold back the inevitable force of nature; she was very close to giving birth.

John wasn't a very practical man, but with his adrenalin running, he knew instinctively that he had to find a way to get Anna off the roof and into the dinghy. The level of water had risen to within two feet of the roof joists, so John shouted to Anna to wait while he swam back to the dinghy. As it happened, the painter was floating on the surface and trailing towards him. He managed to grab it from where it was jammed in the doorway! He tried to haul it free, but it didn't move. Then as if to order, there was another slight earth tremor, and the dinghy was free! And it floated gracefully towards him. He secured the boat and managed to get Anna to slide down the roof and into his arms.

She was very heavy with child, but somehow he managed to lift her and lower her into the dinghy, which nearly turned over, but he managed to steady it with his foot.

Anna was wanting to give birth!

John had no idea how to deal with this as he had never been allowed by the women of the household to be anywhere near childbirth. So, Anna let her natural instincts take control. John managed to catch the boy and save him from the dirty water. He used his sharp knife to cut the cord and took off his shirt to wrap the crying boy and handed him to Anna.

In the tumult of the monster wave, there was a moment of absolute joy at the birth of a new life.

The three of them were sitting in the dinghy, shivering: John, his firstborn, was nestling, trying to get to his mother's breast. This was a new experience for Anna, but instinctively, she let him find her breast.

John was cold, so the best thing to do was to get back to the high ground. He bailed the dinghy out with a kitchen pan that was floating by and found a piece of timber to paddle out of the cottage. He managed to get to the doorway, but the dinghy had to be tipped onto its side to get through. Anna was slipping to the side at the bottom of the boat. The weight of her and the baby was tipping it further over, and it started filling with water again. John was pulling the boat through, using the doorframe.

All of a sudden, the boat was free! But there was still the raging water to contend with, and it tipped over. Anna tried to save herself, but she was slipping out. To save the boy, she almost threw him into John's arms but couldn't save herself. She was carried away, around the corner, away from the cottage and into the mainstream. She managed to hold on to a large piece of a roof which was moving very quickly, being pushed by the surge of torrent.

John managed to right the dinghy, and he tied his shirt into a papoose to hold his newborn son close

THE AUCTION ROOM

to his heart. His only thought was of saving him! He pulled himself hand over hand around the walls of the crumbling cottages. The surge seemed to slacken. St Decumans came into view framed by the walls of the remaining buildings. He knew the only way to save his firstborn was to reach the path to the church. He desperately paddled his way, being accosted by a roof floating upside down like a Noah's Ark, which luckily pushed him in the direction he wanted to go. The dinghy grounded, and John jumped clear onto the solid ground, still holding his son close to him!

Woodcut Somerset tsunami, 1607

(VI)
ANNA

The piece of wood that Anna was holding onto became wedged against a submerged wall. The flow had slackened, so she was able to dog-paddle to a small rock that appeared to be close to dry land. She was getting very cold and shivering uncontrollably. She knew she had to get to her son.

Bethany, one of the fishwives she had been visiting, had managed to get to dry land. She saw Anna struggling and going under and nearly drowning but holding on to an island of ground that seemed to be fast disappearing. Bethany found a net with ropes attached, and she threw the net as hard as she could. Anna was getting very weak; she just about caught it on the third attempt, and Bethany pulled Anna to the path. She picked her up and carried her away from the water, wrapped in her coat, up to the church. John met her and helped carry her to where the baby was being looked after by a parishioner's wife. They were briefly reunited, but Anna was so cold and shivering. She needed to be wrapped in dry, warm blankets, after which she revived a little.

(VII)
PULHAMS MILL, 1607
BRONWYN

After Anna's wedding, Bronwyn became very broody. She had been seeing a yeoman farmer, James Dunn. She knew that Anna had had feelings for him, but she felt that it was a good thing that he had been dumped by Anna as Bronwyn had always been a little jealous of her. James was very good-looking and very suitable. He also was enamoured with Bronwyn. He was approved by Gerald as a man who could take over the Mill. It would be a match made in heaven!

So, Bronwyn became pregnant by him, the marriage bands were read, and the preparations were being made for another wedding.

The news of the Great Flood came, along with the fact that her sister had almost died, and she was still in a very bad way. James found some horses and a lightweight cart and hastened to Wyndham Orchard to bring Anna back to the Mill.

She realised that Anna would be too weak to suckle her boy, and as she was pregnant and had started to produce milk, she was going to wet-nurse her sister's child.

On their way down Wind Whistle Lane, the rain and wind seemed to disappear. As they approached a break in the woodland, the sun came out, and the scene lit up before them was not what they had expected! From a distance and as far as the eye could see, was a great calm lake, with the village roofs poking up here and there, looking just like islands. Steep Holm was cut in half,

Flat Holm had disappeared altogether, and everything looked very battered. James and Bronwyn were shocked at what they saw.

They were at a loss as to how they were going to get to rescue Anna. They cautiously passed the entrance to Nettle Combe House and made their way down the lane until the road disappeared into the water. There was debris of shattered homes and dead sheep, even a half

submerged cart with a drowned horse still between the shafts.

Then out of the woods on the hill came the sound of drunken singing! What looked like a vagabond fell onto the lane and he broke his bottle on a stone. He staggered to his feet, cursing in Welsh and broken English, 'My horse is drowned! How do I get back to my farm? This isn't Wales …!' Then he fell over again, soaking wet and drunk as a lord!

(VIII)
ORCHARD, WYNDHAM
JAMES AND BRONWYN

They had found Anna on an improvised bed in front of a fire in the stair's antechamber. She looked very pale. Bronwyn felt her brow; she was very cold but sweating. Bronwyn carefully prised the baby away from Anna and put him to her swollen beast, and fed him; James picked Anna up and wrapped her in a thick curtain he ripped from a window.

Then James carried Anna outside to the waiting lightweight cart. With Bronwyn, the baby and Anna aboard, James whipped the horse into action, off back up to the hills, to Brompton and the Mill.

John Wyndham chased after them on his best horse, hot on their heels, protesting as he tried to stop them, saying, 'The baby is my son. You can't take him from me.'

James fended him off and ignored him! John tried to stop the cart but failed, so he galloped on ahead and told Eleanor to stoke up the kitchen fire and set a bed for his son and Anna.

(IX)
PULHAMS MILL

When they arrived at the Mill, James carried Anna and Bronwyn, Anna's son, into the kitchen. He laid Anna on the bed in front of a roaring fire.

Anna said, 'My son needs me,' Bronwyn put her son on her sister's breast. Anna was hardly conscious but felt the warmth of her newborn and held him close to her heart.

John tried to take his firstborn boy from Anna declaring, 'I am his father, and if Anna dies, I will take him and find a wet nurse back at Orchard Wyndham.'

Bronwyn was having none of this! She took control and pushed John away, saying, 'Anna is my sister, and I will suckle her son, The baby stopped crying, and there was calm.

Anna pulled Bronwyn close and whispered to her, 'Please, you must love my child and christen him James.' Anna was very pale and was fading fast. Bronwyn put James back to her breast.

Eleanor had sent for the herbalist, Cedricson, from the village. When he arrived, he gave her a warming herbal tea. There wasn't a lot else he could do.

Anna passed away peacefully, but the strength of her spirit was still there at the Mill to look after her son. John didn't seem too upset by Anna's passing. He was more interested and desperate to take his son and go back to Orchard Wyndham, but James prevented him from taking the baby from Bronwyn.

John Wyndham stomped out, saying, 'I now have ownership of the Mill. I will come back to take my son and enforce my lordship.'

CHAPTER 6

Francis Westcott's Story

PULHAMS MILL, SPRING 1914

Kitchener was pointing his finger and telling the miller, Edward Westcott, that 'Every Man should do his duty.'

Francis Westcott, the nephew of Edward Westcott, worked as an apprentice miller for Edward and was only 15 and a half. He was getting very excited about going to fight the Boche. The furthest he had been from Brompton was Dunster and Williton on the coast.

When the recruiting sergeant from The Somerset Light Infantry came with his entourage of soldiers with rifles, smart uniforms and exciting tales of derring-do, Francis loved to hear the stories. He wanted to travel to Devonport, which was where The Light Infantry was based at that time. Devonport was 60 miles away! This would be a big expedition for him! He was told that if he joined up, he would be going to exciting places – places that he had only heard about before.

The recruiting sergeant had questioned him about his age, as you were meant to be at least 18 before you could join the army. Francis lied and said he would be 18 in July. He was a big lad *and although the sergeant knew that he was lying, he hadn't let on.*

This was the norm in 1914 as they were trying to boost the number of recruits. There was a competition between the sergeants to get as many lads as possible to join up, so they didn't ask for proof of age. This was an unwritten policy at the time. Although Francis (Frank) could only just about read and write, he had been told about places like India and South Africa by his grandfather, who had been in the army during the Boer War. He had brought back shields and spears and told tales of the Battle of Rourke's Drift where he had been one of the survivors and awarded a medal for gallantry.

Frank's mother, Elsie, didn't want Frank to go, as her father never came back from the war. She wouldn't talk about it as she really had a good relationship with Frank. She just didn't want to lose her only son in another foreign war!

As for Frank, at the age of 15, he just wanted to get out in the world and away from 'boring country life' to more exciting places with foreign names.

The recruiting sergeants had been picked because they were very good at getting young lads excited about all the foreign 'beauties' that they might meet. Frank didn't need encouragement as he was really tugging at the leash of his family.

His sister Louise, the eldest, and his little sister, Martha, were excited as they knew that when they reached 16 or 17, they would have to marry a local lad. They didn't realise that most of the young men would be going to war and probably would not return! For the time being, the strong county girls like Louise were being asked to do the jobs that the lads would have done.

So, Frank joined up, and Edward Westcott asked Louise to do the job that he had done as an apprentice, which was to help mill grain and deliver flour to Pixton Park in Dulverton.

Frank had been to Taunton, which was an adventure, to sign his allegiance to King and country. He had been issued with his uniform and boots and would be issued with his gun when he arrived at his base in Devonport. The commanding officer of his new regiment (a member of the Acland family) from Dulverton knew that Frank's cousin had a really suitable horse to be requisitioned for the war effort. He had asked Frank to ride his cousin's horse, Dusty, who stood at 18 hands and was a sturdy cob. William (Bill) Gabb had purchased her as a foal five years before. He was very proud of her as she had grown into a fine beast. Bill claimed that she was the best filly in the parish, so he was not best pleased when the sergeant came and delivered the bad news that Dusty was going to be sent to war. But the good news was that Frank was going to be riding her down to Devonport and probably was going to look after her. Frank had been picked as a candidate to be the batman to the CO, Colonel Dru. This meant that Dusty would be looked after as his personal transport. Because Dusty was a cob and very big and strong, she could be used to pull a carriage if need be.

(II)
BROMPTON REGIS, SPRING 1914 VILLAGE GREEN IN FRONT OF THE REMAINS OF BROMPTON MANOR

There was a carnival atmosphere with wives, mothers, sisters, sweethearts and proud fathers, brothers, uncles, and cousins, together with the schoolmistress, Beatrice Wotton, and all but one of the 20 village school children were all there, waving Union Flags to cheer their brave new soldiers on their way to do their duty. The Dulverton Town Band, playing 'God Save the King', with flags flying, were adding to the gaiety and the pomp and ceremony of the day Colonel Dru arrived.

This caused much excitement as the villagers very rarely saw their landlord. He had come to Brompton for this occasion as he had a special interest, as many of the villagers' families had worked for his family for generations. He was keen to encourage them to help in the war effort. Frank Westcott, Jerry Winzor, John How and Jim Davy were all village lads who had joined up at the same time and were there in uniform, lined up, ready to be inspected by the colonel.

The recruiting sergeant, two regular corporals and a private driver had arrived in an army truck with other volunteers that had been picked up in Minehead and Dulverton. They all jumped down to join the ranks of Brompton villagers for the celebrations.

Dusty, Bill's mare, was not used to all these people. All she wanted was to go back to the tranquillity of her normal life. Colonel Dru came over to make friends with her. She didn't want to know. She stamped her foot on the colonel's foot. This caused an awful ruckus …he hobbled off to remove his boot to see if there was any damage. Frank broke rank to assist his new boss and to calm Dusty down. He went to warn him not to take his boot off as if he did, he probably wouldn't be able to put it back on again. Colonel Dru was not very happy but was glad to meet Francis Gadd, his new batman, and to have his help. Frank was hoping that this incident would not sour this new relationship. He helped him to his feet and walked behind him, and managed to get up onto the temporary dais.

The recruits lined up in a raggedy way. The sergeant's first orders:

'By the right, dress! Stand up straight! Come to **attention**!'

He marched over to the colonel and saluted! 'Twelve new recruits for your inspection. Sir!'

Colonel Dru said, 'I am a man of few words. We are going to fight a battle for the honour of the King, country, and the British Empire against the enemies of our country, who, if they are not stopped, will take over the whole of Europe! He and his allies are threatening the borders of the British Empire! They have the ambition to invade our shores!'

'Good luck, and may God keep you safe.'

Helped by Frank, the colonel dismounted and then marched to the end of the line. Frank doubled to the other end, dressed, and stood to attention to be inspected. Inspection finished, the sergeant saluted the officer.

'Right turn! By the right, quick march!'

The band struck up, and the villagers broke into song:

Onward, Christian soldiers,
marching as to war,
with the cross of Jesus
going on before!

Christ, the royal Master,
leads against the foe;
Forward into battle,
see his banners go.

Onward, Christian soldiers,
Marching as to war,
With the cross of Jesus,
going on before!

'Halt.' They halted at the back of the army transport. 'At ease. Dismiss!'

All but Frank, who had been ordered to mount Dusty, clambered into the back of the transport. The colonel saluted them and marched to his open-top Lagonda. His driver ran around and held the rear door open.

Unfortunately, the colonel missed his footing and fell face forward onto the back seat! There was a very subdued, embarrassed titter of laughter from the villagers. The colonel recovered himself and sat very upright as he called Frank over:

'I expect you to ride my horse down to Devonport as quickly as possible. You will be able to break your journey at Upcott Barton, near Cheriton Fitzpaine. Here is a note to give to my cousin, Thomas Fursdon, at Upcott Barton. He will stable my horse. You may well find accommodation at the hostelry, the Ring of Bells, in the village. Don't overtax the horse!' Frank hardly had time to acknowledge and salute the colonel before he told his driver, 'Go now!'

The transport with the new recruits drove off. The crowd lined the road, cheering, singing, and waving flags; mothers and loved ones shed tears. They realised that they might not see their lads again.

Frank dismounted and loaded his backpack, and hugged his mother and sisters. His father man-hugged as he slapped his son on the back. Even he was hiding a tear and wished him, 'God's good luck! Don't let the bastards get you!'

Frank mounted Dusty and cantered off after the transport down the hill to Bampton and followed the droving track towards Crediton.

After an uneventful but very tiring three-day journey, Private Frank Westcott and Dusty, a bay mare cob, were both ready to feed and rest. Arriving at the naval barracks in Devonport, he showed his papers, stabled and fed Dusty in an outhouse to the officer's quarters and was marched to the quartermaster's office to report his arrival to his CO, Lieutenant Colonel Dru. The colonel was not available, so he was marched to the billet for new recruits.

HMS Grand Castle

(III)
THE DOCKS AT DEVONPORT, THREE DAYS LATER

Alongside the King's Wharf was the troopship.

Frank was on the wharf with a well fed but stressed horse. Dusty wasn't used to all the noise and soldiers marching. Frank had trouble keeping her calm. She knew that things were going to happen to her that she wouldn't like. The horses that she had been stabled with were being hauled up and into the monster alongside the wharf. She wanted to go back and stay at home where she was loved and had a peaceful life. Like all waiting to board, she had no choice. The die was cast!

Private Frank Westcott had been given his orders. They were bound for India. He was equally nervous and excited about the adventure ahead. He could not wait to get to the sea and experience new places, food, and people. He was to board the ship and be billeted in the mess nearest to the quarterdeck where he was to exercise Dusty and muck her out. He would have to clean her muck from the officers' deck.

The 11 recruits that he had met in Brompton had been issued with their rifles and kit and were lined up with about 240 other recruits on the wharf while the officers strutted about! The sergeants were shouting, trying to sort out the troops who were struggling, weighed down, and carrying their rifles and kit into a line to mount the gangway in an orderly way up to the deck. Waiting on board, there was another group of sergeants and naval petty officers shouting orders, directing them to their quarters below decks. Many of the recruits looked scared and confused, doubtless wondering what they had volunteered for!

Frank had been ordered to go aboard before the troops to find the place where Dusty, the CO's horse, was going to be stabled for the voyage. He was shown, by one of the sailors, to the purpose-built box stowed just below decks but with easy access to the quarterdeck! Frank had carried some straw up to bed Dusty. As he sorted it out, the colonel came to inspect the billet. He was satisfied and told Frank to go back onto the wharf, adding, 'Make sure that Dusty's straps that are to lift her are arranged properly. I have seen horses dropped onto the deck!!'

Dusty was clearly not very happy and was very restless, kicking out, but when Frank arrived, she calmed down. She trusted him. The straps were arranged, and the lifting began. She relaxed then as she knew the worst was over. There was nothing to do! Frank ran up the gangway to get to the deck to guide Dusty down safely and lead her down into her new home for the sea voyage.

The next day, after all the officers, men, guns, and ammunition were boarded. There was an order to set a parade on the quarterdeck at 8 a.m.

The 250 men who had boarded were being organised by the sergeants and split into sections of 12 men. They appeared as a disorganised, motley crowd, but this was not going to last long. They were given orders to stand to attention and present arms. They were going to have intense training during the voyage of six to eight weeks. On this parade, they were counted and issued with their bedding and sent below to their quarters.

The captain had been given his orders. The next morning the ship was to be ready to sail for Bombay, India.

(IV)
AT SEA

After two weeks at sea aboard HMS *Grand Castle*, Frank was really getting used to his job of looking after Dusty. For the first week, as they passed through the Bay of

Biscay, the weather was really bad. The storm made it very difficult to exercise her; she was very upset as she couldn't get a footing on the deck, and she would slide all over the place! *And* she was seasick. So the best thing was to tie her to the outside of her box for a short time while he mucked her out and kept her tethered to the walls so that she would not lie down. If she did this, it could be fatal, especially if she was unable to get up by herself.

Frank managed to avoid a lot of the 'army bull', but he did still have to do training. When they sailed into the Mediterranean, the weather improved, and the troops were marching up and down, being exercised. Once a week, the sailors would launch a target to trail behind the ship, and each soldier was issued with ten rounds of 303 ammunition and given instruction by the gunnery sergeants as to how to hold and aim their rifles. They needed to get a good score and be able to handle their rifles with safety and confidence by the time they reached India. This was very difficult because the ship was moving with the sea, even when it was calm.

Most of Frank's morning was taken up with either looking after Dusty or attending to the needs of his CO. Being a batman meant that when he had mucked out Dusty and exercised her, he would have to smarten up and then help the colonel to dress for breakfast in the officers' mess.

(V)
WEEK 2
AT SEA IN THE MEDITERRANEAN, JUST OUT OF GIBRALTAR

Over the weeks at sea, this became a very enjoyable routine. The weather in the Mediterranean was very kind to them and it was as if the whole of the ship's company was on holiday, something that the recruits had never had before.

The cooks were a mixed bunch. The chef was from Ceylon, and his helpers were Chinese and Indian, so the food tended to be fairly exotic curries and a lot of rice. Sometimes the curries were far too hot. This resulted in the heads being disgusting. There was a Chinese laundry on board, and one of the Chinese, PouWan, was a tailor, who taught the squaddies how to make and mend.

At times, Frank was permitted to eat the same food as the officers, as his job was to serve it to the CO in his cabin. He developed a taste for wine, and some of the colonel's wines were excellent! When a bottle was opened, there always seemed to be a little left over.

Some of the members of his section were jealous of Frank – in particular, Lance Corporal Jerold (Jerry) Winzor, who was his section leader. He really had it in for Frank. He had history with Frank, and he didn't see why Frank had all this apparent freedom. He reported this to Sub-Lieutenant Boddington, who was very young, green and a 'bit of a wimp'. This was his first assignment, so he referred the complaint up. It was brought to the attention of the colonel! Dru was having none of this. He valued the work that Frank did, looking after Dusty and keeping his cabin tidy and cleaning his brassware.

Although it wasn't normal, he decided to make him up to a corporal. (This usually only happened after about three years of showing leadership qualities. Frank was very young – they thought he was 18, but he had only just turned 16) As you can imagine, this did not go down well with Jerry. Frank was now senior to him; he could come and go as was required.

Things settled down again as they arrived off Malta.

(VI)
WEEK 4
NAVAL DOCKS AT VALETTA
MALTA

The *Grand Castle* couldn't dock at the Albert Dock in Grand Harbour as the battleship HMS *Indomitable* was tied up alongside, so they had to tie up to a buoy in the centre of the harbour. The ship's crew and the squaddies were stocking the ship with guns and ammunition from tender barges. A four-inch gun was installed on the fore-deck. The ship was going to sail fairly close to Turkey and possibly enemy waters! They were setting out that evening for Port Said and the Suez Canal. There was no possibility of shore leave. Only the CO and his batman could go ashore. Again, this was not well received by Lance Corporal Winzor. Frank was in the mess, changing into his No. 1s, preparing to go ashore, when Winzor accosted him.

'Why can you go ashore when none of us can go? You must be the CO's wiffy! It's a wonder you don't share his bed.'

Frank tried to ignore this, but Jerry kept on! Frank faced up to him!

Winzor threw a punch which knocked Frank off his feet; he fell onto the mess table. He wasn't hurt, and he didn't think this warranted a fight. He found his feet, turned his back, and walked away. The CO was waiting for him, but Winzor wasn't satisfied. He picked up a knife, and as Frank turned to go. Winzor shouted, 'You girly boy bastard!' and stabbed Frank.

Three squaddies tried to hold Jerry back, and as Frank fell on his face to the deck, there was a knife still in his back.

Private Jim Davy, who was a schoolmate from Brompton, pulled the struggling Winzor away, and went to pull the knife out.

Sergeant Bull, who had come to see what the fight was all about and stopped him, advising, 'Don't! Wait for the medic.' Then he issued a command 'Private How, go to the wardroom. Find the CO, tell him what's happened and ask Naval Surgeon Lt Bingley to come urgently!'

There didn't seem to be a lot of blood, but Bull knew that if he pulled the knife out, it could be very bad news. Davy found a blanket and covered Frank. Several of the squaddies held Winzor, who was still trying to get to finish the job! The MPs arrived, handcuffed him and frogmarched, pushed and dragged him up the ladder to the main passage and onto the guardroom.

The CO accompanied the surgeon down to the mess. As he arrived, after all the excitement, most of the squaddies were having their breakfast; they stood and came to attention! Lt Bingley was concerned about Frank and decided to send him ashore with the CO to the Royal Malta Artillery Hospital in Valletta. There was a tender standing by, ready to take the CO to a meeting on board the flagship HMS *Indomitable* with Lt General Archibald Murry.

Frank was stretchered and winched down into the tender. Colonel Dru was piped aboard, and they sped off to the wharf. A naval ambulance and the CO's transport were waiting for them. With all this movement, Frank had started to bleed. They needed to get him to the hospital as soon as possible!

Just as the ambulance was leaving the dockyard by the east gate, a grey-haired Maltese man on a bicycle on his way to work turned into the gate, unbalanced, and fell off in front of the ambulance. The driver couldn't stop in time, and although he missed him, he ran over the bicycle. The driver jumped down to see if the man was OK. The bicycle wheel was crushed and bent and lying on top of the worker. His foot seemed to be trapped, and he was shouting hysterically. The driver's mate backed the vehicle off and moved the bike. Joseph, the injured dockyard worker, was bruised; his foot was grazed, and he was really shaken up but otherwise OK!

The crew tended to him, but Joseph was more worried about his bicycle and how he was going to get to work, so the crew bundled him into the ambulance as well. They had almost forgotten about Frank, but they had to get him to the hospital and the new therapy of blood transfusion. Hoping there would be no further drama, the driver put his foot down. Joseph was hopping about accusing the driver (in Maltese) of destroying his bike and ruining his life.

(VII)
ROYAL MALTA ARTILLERY HOSPITAL AMBULANCE ENTRANCE

The emergency crew were waiting with a gurney. The colonel had alerted them to treat his injured batman immediately. Francis Westcott was conscious, but in a very bad way, so he was rushed to the Accident and Emergency Department. Frank was laid on his side. There were three doctors and three nurses attending to him. They tried to attach the blood transfusion kit to him. They couldn't find a vein, the problem being this was a new procedure.

There seemed to be a lot of blood spilling on the floor, being wasted. Eventually, the main man was successful. The knife was very carefully removed. The wound was investigated, and they concluded that, luckily, it didn't seem that any of his vital organs had been damaged.

The atmosphere became more relaxed. He was moved to the attendant ward under observation Frank revived a little. Nurse Sub-Lieutenant Gill Green tried to convince him to relax. All he could think about was that he had to go and tend to Dusty. Gill had no idea who or what Dusty was.

(VIII)
VICTORIA WARD

The colonel had finished his meeting. He arrived at the hospital with his aide-de-camp and enquired which ward his batman was in. It's not very often that an officer of his rank would be visiting an injured squaddie, so there was a lot of scurrying about as the colonel was escorted to the ward. He was concerned and wanted to know why Frank had been stabbed in the back. This was a disciplinary problem in the ranks which was very bad for the morale of the troops, especially as he had just made Frank up to corporal. There was bound to be a court martial, and it would reflect very badly on him and this newly formed troop of very green recruits.

The colonel was to question Frank as to why this had happened! Before he could answer, Frank started to have a fit! The nurses and doctors rushed around to find out what was going on. The colonel stepped away to allow the procedure! Clearly, the doctors had missed something. Frank was rushed back into the trauma room. They were worried that he might have a heart attack. Things calmed down as he seemed to recover and was breathing steadily again.

On his way out, the colonel gave the order that as soon as it was practical, Frank should be taken to the onboard sickbay, telling them, 'The ship is going to sail for Port Said in 24 hours.'

The doctors weren't happy about this, but it was an order, so they tried to find out what was wrong with Frank. There didn't seem to be anything obvious. They concluded it was shock.

The next morning, HMS *Grand Castle* was ready to sail and Frank was stretchered and winched aboard and taken to the sickbay. He wanted to walk, but Lieutenant Bingley wouldn't let him. Just as Frank was being wheeled through to the sickbay, Jerry Winzor was being marched to the wardroom to answer the charges of ABH and attempted murder. He was not at all contrite; he shouted abusively, 'When I get out of the slammer, you're dead!'

The troopship sailed from Valletta Grand Harbour, and the days were very warm. Everything dropped back into an everyday routine

Frank was recovering well and didn't seem to be any worse for the drama. He spent a lot of his spare time with Dusty. Private Pitt had taken Frank's place with the mucking out, but he didn't much care for horses. Dusty had kicked out at him, and he was frightened of her now.

Unbeknown to the crew of the troopship, a German U-boat had been shadowing them, and when they were two days away from Port Said near the coast of Turkey, it was hove to for some maintenance work, almost within spitting distance of them.

The weather was fine, and the crew were feeling in a holiday mood on a beautiful beach. Unfortunately, being a little lax, someone had left some navigational lights on!

That night, a smart lookout on the *Grand Castle* picked out a light on the horizon and informed the watch. The duty officer didn't know what this meant, so he called Captain Coulbourne. As they came closer, he immediately recognised the pattern of lights as a submarine. He knew his only defence was to approach the sub at night and ram it! Better than being sunk with all hands. He didn't have time to consult the colonel. He only had one chance; he had to do it now!

He turned the ship around and headed full steam directly towards the lights. About a mile away, he cut the engines. He had been doing a top speed of 13 knots, using the tide and the silent way the ship had built up.

The troopship hit the sub amidships and rolled it over onto some rocks, which fatally holed the vessel. The crew of the U-boat were completely taken by surprise. Some of them were ashore, and others were scrambling out in the shallow waters. The sub's commander was in big trouble! The reaction was to take a few potshots at this monster that they could only make out as a giant shadow of a ship that had destroyed their U-boat.

Meanwhile, in Cyprus, when Lieutenant General Archibald Murry heard the news, he was not best pleased. His long-term plans for the defence of India had been upset by the action of Captain Coulbourne ramming the U-boat with his troopship, although he couldn't complain too much, as this action made sending troopships through the Mediterranean a lot safer. He decided that the troops should be transferred to an Australian ship, the *SS Omrah* that was offloading troops in Alexandria.

Back off the coast of Turkey, Captain Coulbourne took the ship full astern to extract her. There was a terrible tearing and crunching as the two vessels parted. The troopship had a gaping hole in the bow just above water level, but it wasn't terminal! He decided that he should get as far away and as quickly as possible. The watchman on the bridge turned on a powerful signal lantern spotlight. This lit up the submarine and rescue boats from the shore.

As the Turks were not, as yet, officially at war with the UK, there was no reason to feel that the ship was a risk. But the colonel was taking no chances, and he was keeping the troops on alert. The 4-inch gun on the foredeck was kept loaded and manned.

Captain Coulbourne and Colonel Dru were ordered to meet up with a ship to take the troops off. The order was given to proceed at full speed (about 13 knots). The ship's crew were working hard to try to secure the hole in her bow. They used anything they could to waterproof the first bulkhead, which didn't seem to be badly damaged, but some of the rivets kept popping out, and the crew were replacing them with wooden pegs. The pressure of the water as they moved forward was considerable, the pegs leaking, but the pumps were working hard and seemed to be winning! But this speed could not be kept up for long.

The *Grand Castle* slowed down and limped on slowly for two days away from the coast so that she could meet up for the transfer. The *Omrah* had disembarked troops from Queensland in readiness for the expected campaign against Turkey. She was to take the troops from the damaged ship and then return through the Suez and on to Bombay. The second in command of the 6th Battalion Somerset Light Infantry, a major made up of Lieutenant Colonel Batten, was to take the troops on to India.

The weather was still calm and favourable when the *Omrah* met up, and the transfer was very orderly. The CO and his batman stayed aboard the *Grand Castle* with a skeleton crew and two hefty military policemen. The colonel was going to preside over the court martial of Jerry Winzor in Alexandria. Statements were taken on board the *Omrah* from the squaddies who had witnessed the stabbing. The troopship limped on to Alexandria as it was the closest friendly port that could deal with emergency repairs. The CO and his batman would also go ashore.

(IX)
PORT ALEXANDRIA

The damaged troopship was going into a dry dock to sort the bow out, but the dry dock in Alexandria was too small, so she was to be towed back to Valetta, Malta. Frank went ashore with the colonel to establish him in The Windsor Palace Hotel, which was being used as the senior British officer's accommodation and headquarters.

Frank was to stay in the servants' quarters. Dusty was getting used to being hoisted on and off ships. Frank had to find a stable for him, but there were no army facilities nearby. He was given the task of renting one as near to the quay and the Windsor as possible. Frank was excited and a little apprehensive about trying to communicate in a different language and negotiate in Egyptian francs. He was quite streetwise, but it was a different ball game as this was the first foreign country he had ever been to. A lot of the locals spoke a bit of English because Alexandria was an important resort for the British tourists doing their grand tour. He found that the Hantoor carriage drivers were best. Hammad was particularly helpful as he had a large stable, and he was glad to have an English officer's horse. It was status for him! The price seemed good, so Dusty happily landed and joined Hammad's two horses.

Frank had some time to explore. This was short-lived as when he arrived back at the Windsor, he heard the news that the colonel was to be posted to a new job as commander of a new regiment on the Western Front. An American ship was due in Alexandria and would arrive in Gibraltar in seven days. The colonel, Dusty and Frank were to travel up through Spain by train to France and eventually to the trenches. Frank was not looking forward to that; he'd had a pretty exciting time since he had volunteered. He was missing Brompton, his sisters, and the quiet life, and he was worried about Dusty as he had heard a lot of tales about wartime horses. But there was still a lot of excitement ahead before he returned. He had never travelled on a train before!

The colonel, his batman and his horse were safely loaded, and the *SS Unity* sailed. For a change, the journey was fairly uneventful and, yet again, Dusty was unloaded from a ship. The colonel was whisked away for lunch in a staff car to meet the general. Frank had to ride Dusty over the border to the railway at San Roque-La Linea station in Spain.

When he arrived, the train was due to leave in 15 minutes. He loaded Dusty and gave him a nosebag full of food and then walked the length of the train, but there was no sign of the colonel. Just as he was giving up hope, a staff car swung onto the platform, and the colonel boarded the train with Frank's help and with Frank carrying the bags.

The train steamed away and in three days they arrived in Madrid, where they changed trains; then it was four days to the foot of the Pyrenees with frequent stops for food and water. There were two engines as they were several low-load waggons with tanks and guns on board.

The colonel travelled in a first-class sleeper compartment and was served his food by the catering staff on the train. Frank helped but spent most of his time with Dusty. He did have a bunk in a carriage which he shared with four Spanish civilians – the crew delivering the tanks. In the next compartment, there were some

Spanish railwaymen. Out of all these fellow travellers, only one spoke a little English. So, Frank would eat in the kitchen. At stops, he would exercise Dusty and muck her out.

Frank had spent a lot of time with Dusty. He really loved her and didn't want her to become a war horse! He knew that the train was heading for the British Headquarters in Chantilly, and when they arrived there, Dusty would be offloaded and used to transport supplies to the front. He didn't realise this was never going to happen.

(X)
THE JOURNEY TO THE WESTERN FRONT

The train chugged very slowly, climbing onto the plateaux to the foothills of the Pyrenees and heading at a snail's pace towards Canfranc where they were to stop for at least a day. The loads had to be transferred to narrow gauge waggons and carriages, and prepared to go through the unfinished Somport Tunnel.

When they reached Canfranc, the colonel was to stay that night in the new station hotel. He was to be the first customer. First, Frank had taken the colonel's luggage and sorted out his room for him; then, he found his own accommodation in the servants' quarters. He unloaded Dusty and saddled her up and rode up a path into the mountains. The day was cold but fine, and the air was crystal clear. He felt that life was really treating him well, considering the war had started. But he missed his mates whom he'd joined up with and his family. He wished that Louise, his eldest sister, was here. She and Francis, as she would always call him, had been good friends (she was only a year younger than Frank) and they had explored the Exmoor hills and valleys and climbed trees as children. He knew that Louise would be amazed at the awe-inspiring beauty and the height of the mountains around him. Dusty was really happy to be out of the confinement of the last months. All in all, he would have liked to just keep on this track and not go back to the train. Frank knew he was going to be in trouble with Colonel Dru as he should have been back an hour earlier.

When he arrived back, all hell had broken loose! As they had moved one of the tanks to a different flat waggon, it had toppled off and was stuck at a precarious angle. The 17-ton weight had been too much for the lifting gear. Luckily, there had been such a fuss that he had not been missed. This was going to delay their departure. Dusty was stabled in the new station building until the railway workers had sorted out the tank.

The colonel was keen to get on, but there wasn't anything he could do about it. So, he relaxed and enjoyed his dinner and said to Frank that if he put on his civvies, he could join him. This would not be acceptable under normal circumstances, but there were no other army personnel around. Frank had a good relationship with the Colonel.

Frank was only able to find a white shirt and a jacket. He hoped that people wouldn't notice his army boots. He did feel a little awkward. He had never eaten in a restaurant before, let alone with his commanding officer. He didn't know which knives and forks he should use, but the colonel put him at ease by saying, 'You can't call me "colonel" or "sir" tonight, call me Peter – just for this evening.'

The food came, and they both ate in silence. They were both a little embarrassed. The food was over; Peter asked Frank about his family. Frank opened up; he told him how he missed his sisters and his mother. Peter asked about how Dusty was faring and said that as they were going to be delayed, he would exercise her at ten in the morning and that Frank should find another horse in the village so he could accompany him. The meal was over. Frank was happy to go back to check on Dusty, give her some food and water and get to his bunk.

Early the next morning, he scouted around the village and found Bella, a similar size mare. Frank and Peter mounted and rode up the same track as he had gone the day before. The weather was still fair but with a chilly wind. But by lunchtime, the clouds were gathering, and the wind was blowing through the pass. They turned back as they rounded a large outcrop.

A brown bear appeared, reared up on its hind legs and growled and then disappeared. It gave Dusty a fright, and she reared up, too, so that the colonel lost his seat; he fell and hit his head. Frank jumped down to catch Dusty's reins, but Bella galloped away back home.

The colonel didn't have much luck with Dusty! But he wasn't badly hurt, so Frank helped him on again and led her back to the hotel. The manager fussed around the colonel and said in very broken English. 'What have you done to my only customer!'

Sunday was a day of rest, so the train would be repaired and ready by the Tuesday. At about 10 a.m., the train was loaded with the cargo and Dusty. All aboard!

The steam engines shunted the train onto the narrow-gauge track, and they started the perilous journey through the Somport Tunnel. The tracks had been laid in 1912, but work had stopped because of a disagreement between French and Spanish companies over funding (nothing changes) and the war! The journey was slow and tiresome. The soot and coal, dust and steam were choking as there was no proper ventilation. The tanks were just scraping the sides, but otherwise, the trip was uneventful. Everyone on board was glad to get to Forges d'Abel and the crystal air of the Pyrenees, even though it was raining hard and blowing a gale. Finally, the train stopped for water and fuel.

Frank was able to give Dusty a short exercise and some food and water. He rode along beside the train. He could only just get past the overhanging tanks. The engineers were trying to secure them as it seemed that they had worked loose. He thought to himself that it looked as if the trucks were overloaded. When he had loaded Dusty back in his box, he went to check that the colonel was OK. As he approached his compartment, the colonel was beside the track discussing this problem! He was concerned because the gauge of the track was very narrow; when the train negotiated around the very sharp bends, the tanks could overbalance. The engineers basically couldn't do anything about it!

So when the train had taken on the water, it was all aboard again! The driver did take it very slowly around the bends. It was fairly uncomfortable as the coaches swayed a lot. Frank stayed with Dusty to keep her safe! The travel was again very slow, and there was no one to talk to. Dusty wasn't the best conversationalist, but she was warm and glad to have the company. The days and nights went by.

Somport Tunnel, Spanish Pyrenees

(XI)
BY THE RIVER

The next unexpected stop was along the riverbank under a cliff. The rain was torrential and a few stones started falling, crashing and bouncing on top of the carriages. Then there was a loud rumbling sound of water streaming and rushing out of the sides of the cliff. There was a sudden loud crash; Dusty's carriage shuddered, leaned over to about 20 degrees and then back to upright. Dusty was tied to the wall but lost her footing and nearly crushed Frank, but the box didn't fall off the tracks and righted itself again. Then there was an eerie stillness and just the sound of the engine letting off excess steam. It was obvious that the train wasn't completely derailed. Frank jumped down to survey the scene.

It was pretty much a disaster. The front of the train, the two prime mover engines, the flat wagons with the tanks and the first-class and second-class carriages had toppled over, had rolled down the bank and had ended up on their sides half submerged in the river. Frank's first thought was to get Dusty out of the box and onto the top of the riverbank. He tied him to a post and clambered down to the edge of the river. He could hear people calling for help. He managed to get in the river, which was fast flowing but only waist height. He tried to open the door of the first-class carriage, but the frame was buckled and would not budge. He found a broken window and could see the colonel. His head was above water, but he seemed to be unconscious. He was breathing though, and when Frank said, "Are you OK, he responded with a mumbled, 'Yes! But can you get me out of here? But first, can you see if any of the crew are still alive.'

It was obvious that the colonel was trying to remain in control as he added, 'I'm trapped here, and I can't move my lower half, but I'll be alright for a bit! I thought I heard someone calling in the next compartment.'

Frank struggled along the side of the carriage and found a Spanish man in much the same situation, but he had a very nasty cut on his head and looked as if his neck was broken. He didn't respond when Frank managed to get in and hold his head above water. He tried to pull him free, but he was stuck fast. Frank couldn't feel a pulse, so he assumed that he was dead. There were three more very bloody bodies in the river being washed away. Both of the tanks had broken their securing chains and were lying upside down in the river.

This made it easier for Frank to tightrope walk along the edge to the flat wagons to get to the prime movers. As he got closer, the steam was throwing out boiling water and spraying it over Frank. He couldn't get to see if the drivers were trapped. The coal had mostly fallen into the river. There was a loud hissing and a sizzling noise from the fireboxes as the river put the fires out. As the steam cleared, Frank managed to look in the footplate of the engines but could see no sign of life. On the bank above, there were two crushed bodies. The engines had rolled over them.

The coupling that had linked to Dusty's box and the guard's van had broken; they were the only parts of the train still upright. Frank found a rope and tied it to Dusty's halter and took the other end down, and tied it to the door of the first-class carriage. Then he tugged at it to make Dusty pull. She took just two or three steps, and the door came away and dragged it up the bank a little way. Frank jumped down onto a seat and put his head under water and could see what was trapping Peter's legs. It was one of the other seats that had fallen across him and jammed in the broken window frame. It looked as if it had broken both his legs.

This was going to be a problem, but he again found the end of the rope and pulled it down to the carriage and did two half hitches around the seat and tugged again. Dusty moved gently forward. This pulled it away from Peter's legs as he screamed in pain. Now the problem was how to get him out, as every movement was obviously painful. Frank had found the colonel's hip flask of brandy, so he gave him a couple of swigs to keep him conscious and alert.

He needed to get him really drunk so he wouldn't feel the pain.

He found some useful lengths of 3x2 timbers and some rope and took deep breaths. After six attempts, he managed to straighten and tie the splints to Peter's legs. By now, the colonel was shivering with cold and shock, so Frank gave him more brandy. Then Frank was ready to pull him out. He hadn't had time to worry about himself or about what was going to happen next! He just got on with it, as farmers' lads do! He worked out that if he could get the door down from the riverbank, he could use it as litter. He did this and tied the colonel to it, and with Frank's guidance, Dusty pulled the door out of the carriage and up the bank onto the flat beside the horse box. Thankfully, Peter had passed out. The adrenaline and the brandy had done their job.

Frank tied Dusty up and climbed into the guard's van and found that it was empty. He didn't understand where the guard had gone as he had been there when they left Canfranc. The coal burner was alight, so he managed to drag the litter holding the colonel through the double doors and lay him near the burner. He revived a little, and he stopped shivering. The brandy had helped with the shock; his colour was returning.

Frank left him and went down to find Peter's clothes and equipment. His own gear was all in the horse box. He found some food and coffee in the kitchen next to the first-class carriage, and Peter's luggage. He dragged it all up to the horse box and took the coffee into the van, and made hot drinks.

Then he fed Dusty and brought some water up for her. He put her winter blanket over the colonel and gave him a hot coffee to sip. So much had happened in the last few hours he hadn't noticed the time go by. The rain had stopped and it was getting dark! He realised that he was hungry, so he organised some food for them both, stoked the fire for Peter and bedded himself down in the horse box with Dusty.

(XII)
THE MORNING AFTER THE CRASH ON THE BANKS OF THE RIVER, LE GAVE D'ASPE

Frank woke with a start! At first, he thought he had dreamed the horrific events of the day before. It was dark and warm in the horse box. Dusty was snuffling about and chewing her hay. It took him back to Brompton and his good life there.

Suddenly he was back to reality. He didn't know what the time was or where he was, how far the train was from rescuers.

He splashed himself with water, untied Dusty, opened the sliding door and let the light in, then jumped down and led the horse out onto the siding. He looked in to see how the colonel was faring. He had managed to pull himself up onto the conductor's couch and had found some water. He was looking much better. They had coffee. How were they going to get moving? The colonel tried to get organised, but Frank would have to do all the leg work. He had surveyed the scene and could see that the line was blocked. The rockfall and the tanks were even damming the river. The telephone cables were all down. They seemed to be isolated. There was no obvious way out of this new rockfall valley.

Frank, resourceful as ever, decided that he would have to make a sleigh to carry Peter, so he made one out of the timber that was lying about and devised a harness so that Dusty could pull it. He did a bit of exploring around the river to find the path out so they didn't have to climb over the rocks. In the process, he found all sorts of bits that were useful. Then the brakeman from the train appeared. He had raised the alarm but said in broken English that it would be days before the team could get to the train. He said that the best thing to do would be for him to take a path to the nearest village, which was only two hours walk away. So, he helped Frank to set up the drag of two poles and a door to move the colonel.

They set off with Dusty harnessed with bits of leather from the first-class carriage seats. The path was strewn with rocks that he had to remove, and progress was very slow. It was going to take more than two hours! The brakeman went on ahead.

The path through the Pyrenees

They had to stop to eat some bread that he had brought them. Then the weather clamped down, and they had to almost feel their way. The colonel did have a compass in his pack, so they thought they were going in the right direction, but the path didn't go where they wanted to go. Then the path divided and when the weather cleared for a short time, they found they were on the edge of a precipice with a 1,000-foot drop on one side and a cliff on the other! Luckily there was a path that led the way up and away, and above, a rock fell with a torrent of a waterfall coming out of the cliff, which had washed away the path along the precipice. Dusty just kept on pulling the litter up. She would do anything for her Frank.

Almost blinded by the mist, they had no choice but to keep going up. Then they rounded a bend in the path, and suddenly the mist cleared. They had a clear panoramic view of France. They could see plains with farmland and a city that Peter said was probably Lourdes. It seemed like a miracle! It was a struggle to get down from their viewpoint, but it didn't take long, as it was all positive. They felt that they had survived the worst. Frank did wonder what had happened to the Spanish brakeman. The main thing was to get the colonel to a hospital and get Dusty bedded down for the night. They soldiered on until they came to a farmhouse.

(XIII)
FRANCE, 15 KM FROM PAU, NOUVELLE-AQUITAINE

Monsieur Fàbrega was in his yard tending to some goats. He saw the raggedy party (he had heard about the train disaster), and he warned his wife to get a couch ready and to prepare some bread and chabròl for them. He moved the hurdle to let them into the yard and took Dusty's lead rein. Between them, they carried the colonel in and laid him by the fire. They managed to sit him up against the wall, and Madame handed him a bowl of her wholesome broth. Frank stabled Dusty and fed and watered him. Monsieur Fàbrega boarded his very old rusty bicycle and rode down the track to his neighbour, the *maire*, who had a phone. He had heard about the train disaster.

An hour later, a staff car and an ambulance arrived to take Colonel Dru and his batman, Corporal Westcott, to the hospital. But the colonel said that Frank should stay at the farm and ride Dusty to the British HQ in Pau when they were rested. Colonel Dru then instructed the army escort to pay the farmer for the cost of stabling and Frank's board and give Frank some francs for expenses.

Frank was really at home here. He dropped back into being a farm boy. He was happy helping Florance and Phillipe around the farm. They had a hard life, but it was very familiar as it was much like his home in Brompton. Days went by and he almost forgot he was in the army.

One day, a dark-haired lass knocked on the door just as Frank was going to milk the goats. He tried to communicate with the little French he had picked up. It didn't matter, though, as there was an immediate attraction. As he took the bucket that Eloise (for that was her name) had brought for goat milk, their hands touched and they both felt the hairs on the back of their necks tingle. They looked at each other and realised this was something special! They were both young and beautiful.

Eloise took the full bucket and ran off home a kilometre away. Eloise was the daughter of the *maire*, Monsieur Jean-Luc Pestone. He was very protective of his daughter and was not very happy when Frank stopped at the gate. Eloise was in their yard feeding the ducks for foie gras. Frank had never seen this before. He dismounted on the pretext of watching. He needed to touch her, but he was shy. He just stood as close to her as she would allow. She smiled, and her face lit up. They couldn't keep apart.

But, just then, her father, who had been watching, came out to warn Frank off. He thought quickly and asked if he could use the phone to call the hospital to find out how the colonel was.

The *maire* showed him the phone. Frank called the hospital in Pau, but they said that Colonel Dru had been moved by military transport to the British Army HQ in Le Touquet. He asked if there had been any messages left for him, but they didn't understand what he was saying. He gave up and was ushered away from Pestone's daughter, but she came to the gate as Frank mounted. He leaned down and touched her cheek, and she stroked his finger that slipped away as she tried to grab it as he rode off.

Pestone was very unhappy about this, and he called the police and said that there was a British deserter living next door to him. Eloise, who had learned basic English, heard her father on the phone and, on the pretence of going for a walk, ran to tell Frank what her father had done. This put Frank in a difficult position. He had no papers to prove that he was doing what the colonel had told him to do. He packed his kit, thanked Phillipe, and paid him for the extra bed and board out of the little cash in francs he had left. He mounted Dusty and was about to ride away, but Eloise begged him not to go. She gave him directions to a cave he could hide in, and she would join him the next day. Frank didn't have time to argue, so he rode off, following Eloise's directions. For a while, he got lost, but by good fortune, he ended up in the cave that Eloise had described.

(XIV)
BRITISH ARMY HQ IN LE TOUQUET

Colonel Dru had been transported to the medical centre at the HQ and had been in traction for two weeks. He was getting very fed up with the lack of activity. When his next in command asked him who his batman was, he remembered that he had left Pau without having given instruction to have Corporal Westcott and Dusty to be transported to join him. Captain Bolivian, the colonel's right-hand officer, had been trying to find out where Westcott was, but the colonel could not recall the name of the farm where Westcott had been billeted.

He was virtually unconscious when he arrived in Pau, and the British army base there had now been closed down. They just hoped that Westcott would contact Le Touquet as, if he didn't, he would be treated as a deserter and summarily shot on sight. Although the colonel tried to talk to the military police, they were convinced that he had deserted. He wrote to his CO, but he wouldn't listen, so he wrote a letter to General Haig. But he was planning a major offensive and couldn't be bothered with detail such as this! A report came in from the Pau police that there was a British soldier in their area, but because of poor language communication, it was discounted as gossip.

The cave entrance

(XV)
A CAVE NEAR DE LYS, NOUVELLE-AQUITAINE

Frank had found the cave that Eloise had told him about. It was very large, and it had been used as winter shelter, so there was hay and food for Dusty. Phillipe had given him food, some of his wine and unfermented apple juice.

Just as the light was fading, Eloise arrived on a rickety old bicycle. She said in charming franglais, 'I'm leaving home and coming with you.' Even though he really wanted her to come with him, he knew that it would be bad for them both as her father would pull out all the stops to find them and take her back. But he was really glad to see her, and they embraced and bedded down in the straw. The night was a little chilly, but they were warm together.

As they were both virgins, this was a wonderful experience. They clung together in an embrace all night. In the early morning light, they made love for the third time. They slept late and woke to the sound of dogs barking. They quickly pulled themselves together, sure that it was either Eloise's father searching for her or maybe the police looking for Frank. The sound faded away, so they decided not to move for a while. Frank wanted Eloise, his new love to come with him, but he didn't want her to be involved in his problems. As he rightly thought he might be considered to be a deserter and be arrested or even summarily shot. Eloise was having none of this. She protested that she would go with him anywhere. It was very sad that they had met under these circumstances, as they really wanted to be together.

Eloise's father, Monsieur Jean-Luc Pestone, was frantic with worry as she had been out all night. He had a good idea that she had eloped with that *'anglais inconnu fuyard'* and he was determined to find them. He also wanted his bicycle back, as he had crashed his car on the way back from the café the night before (a little too much absinthe). The dogs were no use, so he phoned the police and demanded that they search for the fugitives. They said that they wouldn't start a search for 24 hours. Pestone shouted at them, but to no avail; he was the *maire*, after all.

Frank on Dusty, accompanied by Eloise on the bicycle, rode to another village and made a phone call to Le Touquet; he wanted to speak to the colonel. The connection was really poor. *Le postier* recognised Eloise and asked about her father, so Frank convinced her that she should go home. They left hurriedly and out of sight had a lingering, loving, parting embrace. They didn't want to part, but it was for the best. Her father was bound to catch up with them when Madame phoned him. Frank rode off at a canter; he set his sights on getting to Le Touquet before they arrested him.

(XVI)
THE RIDE FROM THE VILLAGE OF ARUDY TO SAINT-JEAN-DE-LUZ

Frank found out that it was 700 km (450 miles) to Le Touquet. Being from England, he didn't understand the distances in France, so he asked how far it was to the nearest coast. Frank decided it would be best to travel by boat. That way, he would avoid the police. He had picked up quite a lot of French and knew that the sea was *la mer*. He phoned HQ again and managed to speak to the colonel's adjutant, who said that he should go to the nearest police station and give himself up as he was a deserter. He tried to explain what had happened and that he should talk to the colonel, but the captain didn't want to be told what to do by a corporal; Frank gave up and rang off! He decided he would make his own way. He set off for the coast with the plan to find a fishing boat to take Dusty and him around the coast. It took him four days as he had to feed and water Dusty along the way and had to take tracks off the main road. He found the farmers were very generous and let him stay with Dusty in their barns. Farmers' wives would take pity on the handsome lad and share the families' food with him.

(XVII)
FISH QUAY, SAINT-JEAN-DE-LUZ

Frank was on the quay talking to Jean-Claude, who was keen to help as his boat was big enough to take Dusty. The problem was that Frank had no money. Jean-Claude was willing to take him, but he needed money for fuel. Frank was going around the businesses asking for work. But because he was in army clothes, he was getting suspicious looks! He sensed the people felt that he should be in the trenches.

Just as he was getting very despondent, he turned a corner onto the quay, and Eloise nearly ran into him on her bicycle. He thought he was having a vision! She was in tears of joy as she jumped off and fell into his arms with a, '*Bonjour, ma chéri! Enfin je t'ai trouvé.*' Hello, my darling. At last I've found you!

Frank was full of questions. 'How did you get here, my love? Is your father following you? Did you come on the bicycle? You must be tired. Where did you stay? How did you know where to find me?'

The words tumbled out of Eloise's mouth in French that Frank didn't understand. They held on to each other forever until the fishermen started whistling, 'Ouh là là!' The baker's boy, carrying pastries into a restaurant, was so interested that he walked into the door post, spilling the fresh croissants on a table, and knocking cups of coffee over the customers. Everyone was laughing. They helped sort out the embarrassed lad and sat down at another table.

Eloise told Frank how she had said to her father that she was going to visit her aunt, and she had taken a bus. Her aunt had told her that a soldier on horseback had stayed a night in her barn. The next day she had borrowed her bicycle, and here she was! When she declared, 'I am coming with you on the boat! I took 100 francs from my father's stash that he was saving to send me away to the Le Lycée. I am going to pay the fisherman. We will go together,' Frank didn't argue. His love was with him.

(XVIII)
THE FISHING BOAT IN THE BAY OF BISCAY, PAS-DE-CALAIS

The weather was set fine in autumn, and there was a fair wind from the south, which meant that Jean-Claude could save fuel and set sail in *La Lunette* at about 4 knots up the coast as he wanted to fish off Brest. Dusty was getting used to being at sea; the quicker she got there, the better. Jean-Claude knew that the weather could change at any time, but there was high pressure over central France that pushed them on. Jean-Claude was going to pick up some new fishing gear in Le Croisic. Dusty could be exercised, and Frank could get some civvies, and Eloise needed a new dress. They did think of going overland, but there could be a chance that they would be picked up. They bought some wine and bread and returned to *La Lunette*. They left the next day; the weather was still set fine, so Jean-Claude sailed out to sea and into the Channel.

Three days later and they were only a few miles from the English coast. They could see Portland Bill. They were fishing just close to the Portland Race for about three hours when the wind got up and the boat was blown into the Race. It was as if there was a force nine gale. Jean-Claude was very apprehensive as it was getting dark, and he was a long way from home; he decided to shelter in Portland Harbour.

They were running before the wind with a lot of canvas. Just as they jibbed, there was a freak wave that knocked them over. Frank managed to release Dusty and grabbed Eloise by the hand as the boat turned over completely.

The wave was gone, but all the gear was a floating, entangled mass. Most of the catch was back in the sea. Jean-Claude managed to grab Dusty's lead and hold her, releasing her from the net over her head that was pulling her down. Frank dived under the upturned boat to see if he could find a way of uprighting her. He seemed to be underwater for a long time, and Eloise was in tears, hanging on to Jean-Claude and Dusty. She thought Frank had drowned, but they heard a knocking.

He was in an air pocket, and the fishing boat was still afloat, although upside down. A flare went up, and showers of sparks in the sky told them that the coastguard had seen them. They were getting very cold, but all they could do was hang onto the upturned boat. Dusty wanted to swim away. They managed to hold onto her for a while, but she was too strong; her instinct was to make for the shore. Eloise held onto her and was dragged with her. They disappeared into the dark. But by now, Jean-Claude could hear the putt-putt of the lifeboat approaching. The wind had dropped, the tide had turned and was now washing them towards the harbour.

Jean-Claude pulled out a bung in the hull and shouted to Frank, 'Hello! They come,' but Frank didn't reply.

He had surfaced on the other side of the boat and seen Eloise being dragged along by Dusty. He swam after them, but, being a country boy, he had never learned how to swim. He could only doggie-paddle and although he was very strong, he couldn't catch up with them. He was very cold and was becoming exhausted, but he was past the point of no return. He kept on, determined to get to his love. He did reach the shore, and Eloise heard him call her as Dusty pulled her out of the sea.

She ran to him and tried to resuscitate him, lying with him and urging, 'Please! Please don't leave me, my love! Stay with me forever! I want you to be there when I have your child.'

He revived a little, opened his eyes, made an enormous effort to hold on to Eloise, and then faded fast. She tried to warm him with her tears. They were still lying together for what seemed like hours when Jean-Claude and his rescuers arrived.

(XIX)
PULHAMS MILL, NOVEMBER 1914

Colonel Dru came to Pulhams Mill to celebrate the life of his batman in his Lagonda Sports car that had been specially converted so he could drive it without the use of his legs. The Pyrenees train accident had made it impossible for him to be on active service. He was working with the War Office in London. He had finally cleared Corporal Francis Westcott's name. Although Frank had died on the beach in Portland, until a week before, he had been treated as a deserter. The colonel had cut through the red tape to save the reputation of the man who had saved his life. Edward Westcott, Frank's uncle, wanted his brother's son to be buried at the Mill, but the family were non-conformists, And the Methodist chapel was not yet completed.

Monsieur Jean-Luc Pestone had arrived to find his daughter Eloise. He had travelled to Brompton Regis to take her back to Pau. Eloise explained that she was pregnant with Frank's child and wanted to stay, live, and work at the Mill and bring his son up in England.

Monsieur wasn't happy about this, but his wife, Sabine, convinced him that it would be best all around. So, after a service in St Mary's, the cortege arrived at the Mill, and Francis Westcott, aged 17, was to be buried as a hero of the First World War – at Shinning Stone.

The colonel was greeted by Frank's family; the whole village turned out. Most of the locals knew the story, but Colonel Dru needed to tell the world. He was lifted in his wheelchair onto a hay wain.

'Corporal Francis Westcott, Frank to those who knew him, although he never got to the front, was nonetheless a hero! If it had not been for him, I would not be here today. He sadly died in the arms of his first and only love, Eloise. Very sadly, he will not be able to see his son, due to be born very soon. Frank and Dusty, our trusty mare, saved my life by sheer determination.'

CHAPTER 7

Jerry Winzor's Story – Part 1

PULHAMS MILL, ENGLAND, JULY 1919

The Mill had fallen into disrepair over the years. The need for grain and flour locally had waned as the big mills in towns could be more competitive and deliver to farms and bakers.

Eloise had run the Mill after the Westcotts had died, and Frank's son, Francis, was brought up there. Eloise never remarried, although she did have a lot of offers as she was a very handsome woman. One was from a man who she didn't know, but he said that he had been on the *Grand Castle* troopship in the Med. His name was Jeremy Winzor.

Jerry was from Brompton. His parents, Ivy and Fred, had lived at Ditch Farm, but they had both died of Spanish flu in 1918. They had always seemed to live life on the edge of the village in more ways than one. When Jerry was released, he found the untenanted farm in ruins. The fact that Jerry had been in prison for stabbing a fellow soldier didn't help; for some reason, no one told Eloise about Jerry's history, and most of the other lads from the village never returned. The local people, particularly the parents and loved ones of soldiers who had been lost in the trenches, felt that Jerry Winzor had deliberately avoided going to the front. This made him a coward!

He was good-looking and about the same age as Frank. He told Eloise that they had been friends since childhood (which was nearly true), but Jerry was a bully, and he and Frank had had a falling out over a lad whom he had picked on, Peter Gadd, who was Frank's cousin. Frank had taken his cousin under his wing and made Jerry look small in front of the other lads in the village, and Jerry never forgave him for that.

Eloise didn't know all this. Jerry could be very charming and was a ladies' man. He would do anything for Eloise, and their relationship soon developed. Eloise wasn't looking for a new man to replace Frank, but she needed help in the Mill. Francis (Frank's son), who was now three years old, was frightened of Jerry. Although he was very young, he picked up on Jerry's hate and anger and would hide away from him. He wouldn't even eat at the same table.

So, this was not a match made in heaven. But Jerry persisted and became indispensable. He needed a job and somewhere to live and felt that Eloise owed him as Frank had caused him to be court-martialled. In fact, had he had to go to the front, he would have probably been killed in the trenches, but he didn't see it that way. His attempts to seduce Eloise were a way of getting back at Frank.

Jerry had spent many months in an Egyptian prison and was then sent to a prison in the UK. He was supposed to be released to go to the Western Front. But in wartime malaise, his papers were lost, and he remained in Winchester Prison, which was a civilian prison. In 1918 he was released as the authorities didn't know what to do with him. He was luckier than the others he joined up with, but for all that, Jerry was a bitter man.

Eloise was never short of helpers. But they didn't last long when they realised that there was no chance of anything more than a working relationship. Jerry persisted, and although Eloise wouldn't marry him, he managed to become the only man she needed. Until one day, Gregory Gadd (Peter Gadd's father) told Eloise that Jerry had stabbed Frank in the back on board the *Grand Castle* troopship and that he was only interested in bedding her to get back at Frank, who had defended his son when they were lads.

Although he was much older than her, Gregory Gadd was very much smitten with Eloise. It was never going to go anywhere, and he knew that. She was the most eligible lady around, and he was a good friend and helper to her, but she didn't take the story too seriously. He was very protective of her in a fatherly way, and Eloise really missed her mother and sister, but particularly her father.

That night Eloise confronted Jerry with this tale. He managed to talk his way out of it; he said that everyone hated his family. There was a long history of the Winzors being outsiders and incomers. He managed to get Eloise to feel sorry for him. He began to cry, and Eloise, who seemed to be beguiled by this man, comforted him and gave him a hug, which he turned into an embrace. Eloise was still a young woman and she had had no sexual encounters since Frank! She was in need and wanted to be loved and, more than anything, to be touched. Her need seemed to overcome the truth that she had been told by Gregory. Jerry took advantage of her tenderness towards him and turned the whole thing around!

There they stood together in an embrace, he with one arm around her and the other between them. As she hugged him, he moved his hand to touch her nipples through her dress and pressed his lips to her mouth in a kiss and pushing his tongue past her teeth. She didn't resist as she was so in need of tenderness and love. She allowed him to press forward. His hand slowly moved down to her crotch and very gently at first massaged her pubic hairs. Eloise was getting very turned on and Jerry took full advantage of this, pressing his body against hers. With his fingers in her knickers, he massaged her, at the same time rubbing his hard member on her leg. He was not going to stop now. They both needed sex.

Eloise hesitated as she suddenly realised what she was doing. But as far as Jerry was concerned, this was it. They were going to have sex. He let his trousers drop to the floor, pushed Eloise against the wall, lifted her dress and pushed hard between her legs. He lifted both her legs and pushed them apart so she was open for his member. Pushing aside her pants, she didn't resist as, at that moment, she was up for it. He pushed forward, rubbing her, and then tried to enter her with one big push. Eloise pulled away and managed to get her feet back on the floor to escape from him before he pressed home his control over her by making her pregnant. She realised in that second that this was not about any sort of love or even lust. It was about control and revenge.

As it happened, just at that moment, the door to the wheel room opened, and 3-year-old Francis came in looking for his mother. This quickly changed everything! Eloise managed to push Jerry away, with all the strength of a mother, to protect her son and escape from his clutches. Francis ran to her and tried to defend her against this monster interloper. Jerry tried to regain his dignity. He lashed out at Francis, but because his trousers were still around his ankles, he fell flat on his face with his private parts still hanging out and his bare ass in the air. This made him very angry as he could do very little. He was finding it very difficult to even stand up.

He might have seen the funny side of this ridiculous situation, but in fact, it just made him angrier.

Eloise took her little 3-year-old out of harm's way into the next room.

She then returned to help Jerry to his feet. As she took his left arm to help him up to a standing position, he swung a punch with his right fist, which knocked Eloise off her feet. Jerry picked up his trousers and fastened his belt. Eloise was on the floor where he had knocked her down, and as she lay there helplessly, he kicked her in the crotch and ripped her dress. While she was on the floor, he was going to rape her, but plucky little Francis returned behind him and gave him a kick between his legs that hit his vitals and he cringed in a pile.

Both Eloise and Francis escaped into the next room and barred the wheel room so that when Jerry recovered, he would find that he was imprisoned. Her dress was torn, so she picked up a flour sack for warmth and tied it around her with a rope, gathered up her son in her arms and ran up towards the village. As she reached the waggon works, Gregory was walking towards the Mill.

She blurted out, 'He's locked in the wheel room. He'll get out of there and come after me!' Then, in her terror, she reverted to French. '*Il était hors de contrôle!* He's out of control! *Aidez-Moi!* Help me! You can see he's ripped my dress! I can't go back to the mill! *Je dois retourner auprès de mon père en Pau*. I'll go back to my father in Pau.'

Eloise was so very ashamed that she had let this affair go this far. She knew that she had been partly to blame for allowing Jerry to get this close. But she was a lonely woman, and he had played on her vulnerability and loneliness. She had not realised that he was an arrogant psychopath. Although she didn't know how to define him, she was streetwise enough to know that it meant that he felt no guilt. She was now very worried that when he managed to escape – it was going to take him a while as there were no windows, and the door was very heavy oak and barred with an ironclad four-by-five oak beam – he would attack her and harm Frank's son. She had finally realised that his main interest in her was revenge.

Gregory hugged Eloise and reassured her that he and the village would protect her from this 'madman'. He took Francis by the hand with his arm around her shoulders, hugging her close and walking with her to the church, which was the nearest place of safety. Gregory was the churchwarden and key holder. They went through the main oak door, which he then barred behind them. He guided Eloise and her son into the sacristy and sat them down so they could recover from this drama. Eloise was in tears and held on to Gregory and her son for dear life. She took some time to calm down! Gradually the fear and tears subsided into sobs of French and English! *'Veuillez nous protéger de ce monstre!'* Please protect us from that monster!

Gregory tried all he could to calm them down. He said he would have to leave her to go and alert the local policeman. But he would go first and alert his brother's widow – who lived in Broom Cottage just below the church.

'I will leave you for only a few minutes. I'll get Betty to come up and keep you company while I find Constable Pilkington. I saw he'd returned from Dulverton on his bicycle a little while ago. Stay calm; we will protect you. I will lock this door and give the key to Betty. I don't think Jerry has managed to escape yet. But you never know what an angry man might do. Don't let anyone in through the main door. I'll be as quick as I can.' He left and locked the door into the sacristy behind him.

Betty was standing at the door of Broom Cottage, wondering what all the fuss was about. When Gregory told her that Eloise was in the church and had been attacked and raped by Jerry Winzor. She took the key and ran out breathlessly as fast as she could to the sacristy door and unlocked it, and Francis came running towards her. She scooped him up and held him to her ample breast. She closed the door and locked it on the inside. Eloise came into her arms as well. She nearly knocked poor motherly Betty over.

Pilkington arrived and stood on his dignity as the local law, but Gregory was having none of this, declaring, 'There's a serious problem here. We must gather a few of the village men. There's Freddy, "Bull" Burt, Gedd and Davy from Holm Farm, all big men; I'll go and knock them up.

'We'll go down to Pulhams Mill and take this man who's attacked a woman and her son. He's a convicted madman who stabbed Frank Westcott! He needs to be locked up, and the key thrown away!'

PC Cecil Pilkington tried to take control of the situation, but he left it up to Gregory to go knocking on doors to collect the four men who would take no nonsense and had the muscle to sort out Winzor. It was about five o'clock and late spring. All except Gregory had had their dinner and a jug of beer. They marched down to the Mill with Pilkington shouting orders that none of them took any notice of.

Jerry was banging on the door, still in a rage! The gang knew how to deal with him, though. They stood on either side of the door, and Pilkington removed the oak bar. The door flew open, and Winzor came rushing through. Freddie put his foot out and tripped him, and before he could get up, the four villagers sat on him. Pilkington handcuffed him! They frog-marched him up to the church and threw him into the lockup at the bottom of the church steep.

Pilkington was very pleased with himself as he was the constable and the problem had been sorted on his patch. He got on the phone with his sergeant to report how he had solved this serious crime. Then he wrote up his report of how he had organised this without having to call for reinforcements. Sgt Dave Beckman sent a Black Maria from Minehead with three burly PCs to pick up Jerry Winzor.

He was making a lot of noise, banging, and shouting threats and cursing the whole village. The transport took about an hour and a half to get to Brompton, and it was getting dark when they arrived. By this time, he had calmed down and went with the police as quietly as a kitten.

It was only when he left that Eloise would come out of the church. Gregory walked Betty, Francis and Eloise to Broom Cottage and Betty fussed about in her kitchen, making tea. Eloise and Francis were still very shocked, but after a little while, she pulled herself together. By this time, Francis was tucking into the scones that Betty had just made for tea. The lads, who had sorted Jerry, called in one by one on the way to The George to see if she was OK. Gregory was there already and had set up the beers for them as a thank you! There was a lot of banter about how Gregory was hoping that this might work in his favour with Eloise. As much as Gregory would have liked that, he knew that the die was cast. Eloise could not stay in Brompton. That night, she and Francis stayed in Betty's spare room.

In the morning, she went down to the Mill and packed her few belongings and her memories and returned to Betty's to pick up her son. They walked down to Dulverton and took a train to the coast and then found a fisherman in Weymouth who would take them across the channel to France. And that's how the Mill was left to become a ruin.

(II)
PULHAMS MILL, 1934

Years of neglect. The Mill had been left deserted and unloved to fall into ruin. The villagers just used the ground and sheltered cattle in the main part. Nobody seemed to care about the crumbling stone building. The workings were still complete, and the millpond above the overshot wheel and all the grinding stones were there. But the leat had become very overgrown. It was impossible to battle your way up to the weir; the water had been diverted back to the river, the holding ponds were dry, and aller (grey alder), willow and blackthorn trees were growing to about 3 to 4 inches in diameter.

One very stormy night in October 1926, slates were blown off, and torrential rain and wind battered the stone building for several hours. At about three in the morning, a big part of the roof was torn away; it looked like it would be the end of hundreds of years of life and work at Pulhams Mill. Over the next ten years, there were attempts by the village elders to get the owners to put the place back together, but there was a depression. A couple of adjoining farmers put up some corrugated iron to replace the slates, and this stopped the walls from collapsing. Nobody had any money particularly to spend on a ruin that had no apparent use anymore. There were a lot of industrial workers, single men, who had no support from the dole. They became tramps and hitched trains to the country, hoping to find farm work. A few ended up in Somerset.

One such was walking to Land's End, getting lost and arriving in Brompton looking for work and a place to stay. As part of Gregory's duties as churchwarden, he would check on the church, and that's where he found Bertie dossing down on the church porch. He suggested that he shelter down at Pulhams Mill, which was deserted, and got him some work with the wheelwright.

Gregory was a key worker with John How, who ran the building side of this prosperous little village business, which had built the church at Upton and also made coffins. Importantly they were very well known for making carts and hay wains for most of the counties all around. They were one of the last of a long line of wheelwrights; they would paint the waggons different colours depending on which county they were made for.

Since the war, the wheelwright business had all but disappeared. They could saw their own timber and do metal work, and they would do most of the forestry work within a 10-mile radius. They still had building and maintenance work in very hard and changing times. Bertie was quite skilled as he had previously worked as a factory maintenance man in Port Talbot, just on the other side of the Bristol Channel. He had all sorts of skills, from bricklaying to carpentry. As a lad, he had worked with his father, who was a farrier. The How brothers were very pleased to employ an all-rounder like him, and he felt himself lucky to find a job as there were many on the edge of hunger and deprivation. There were whole families with no way to keep body and soul together. He knuckled down, and although the Hows couldn't pay very much, they still had a fair amount of work from the local Pixton Estate. Bertie was very useful, as most of the jobs these days were small and difficult. They were the odd jobs that had to be done to keep the properties together.

Bertie made the best of living at the Mill. It wasn't much, but he managed to get the range working. There was plenty of kindling, and he found an axe to chop logs so he could cook. And he was given a whole bundle of shearing waste wool. He used this to keep himself warm by lining the corrugated iron roof. The Hancocks, who owned the Mill now, felt that it was better that it was occupied but couldn't be bothered with rent. Bertie was keeping the old place alive! He did have the feeling that there was a spiritual presence there, but it didn't seem to be much of a problem. Every now and then, he would hear the sound of dice being thrown or see a shadow pass and then be gone. It seemed that the presence was glad to have company.

Bertie settled down to an everyday life in a very friendly village. He only had an elder sister in Wales as his father, Gareth, had died in the trenches in 1916. His mother had died in childbirth when he was young. Such a shame; he had always wanted a brother to play football with! He had turned into a bit of a loner. He would go up The George pub on a Sunday after church and have a pint of stout and a chat, but he felt a bit of an outsider. He worked hard and kept himself to himself.

On his return to the Mill one Sunday, there was a bloke in rough-looking khaki army trousers sitting in the Mill as if he owned the place. Bertie was taken aback. Then he said that he used to live here with the French woman and used to run the Mill a few years back. He said he was a villager and that his parents, who were lifetime tenants at Ditch Farm, had died, so he was going to move into the Mill! He finally added, 'My name is Jerry Winzor, and I may as well tell you that I was wrongly accused of attempted rape and went to prison. I'm going to move in here until I find other lodgings!'

Bertie didn't know what to do. He couldn't refuse as he had no right to live at the Mill, anyway! So, he said he had better find some furniture as he only had the bare essentials, adding, 'You will have to sleep on the floor, as you certainly aren't going to share my bed. It's too small anyway! How long do you want to stay?'

Jerry was being very arrogant and aggressive. Bertie had always found the villagers very helpful, and they had taken him in as a local, so this was a new side of the village that he was not prepared for. Jerry knew what he was doing, as again, he felt he had the right to walk over people.

Bertie played it cool and said he was going to go up to get some eggs from Holm Farm before they sat down to lunch. He hurried up the road to see John How to ask his advice. John had a phone. His reaction was to ring John Hancock. He knew that the Hancocks wouldn't take any nonsense. But he couldn't get hold of John as he was out. So, he advised Bertie to play it cool for the time being as Jerry was well known for being very violent.

Time went on …

Jerry did do a bit of work on the Mill to make it more habitable; he was quite handy and made a bed and stole some old chairs from the church. While in prison, he had worked in the kitchen and so he did the cooking for both of them when the mood took him. He had soon established himself at the Mill.

Bertie got on with most people. Although Jerry had a temper, he had mellowed. He managed to get some work around the village, mostly from his parents' friends who knew Jerry and felt for Bertie. Jerry and Bertie seemed to be getting on, but the locals were a little frightened of Jerry. He was very unpredictable.

New bungalow

(III)
PULHAMS MILL, 1938

At a village dance, Bertie met up with Joyce Hancock (youngest sister of John, owner of the Mill.) They had a brief courtship and married in St Mary's that spring. They moved temporarily into one of the How's cottages. John Hancock decided to build a modern bungalow on the tumbledown site at Pulhams Mill. John Hancock managed to get Jerry to move on as there was a war brewing in Europe.

Jerry was getting very restless, and he decided to go to France to avoid the call-up. His ego was such that he had the strange idea that if he found Eloise. she would need him, and he could carry on the relationship that he had dramatised while in prison. He had built it up into a love story with her 20 earlier.

Bertie and Joyce settled down to live and work in the new asbestos and wooden bungalow that Joyce's brother had built for them. It had a new Rayburn, which meant that they had heating and constant hot water, and they put in a telephone. It had two bedrooms and a kitchen with a pantry at the rear and a brand-new log fire in the lounge.

They farmed about 30 acres and had 12 cows. This gave them enough milk to fill a couple of churns. When they started, they milked by hand. They had a few chickens and a dozen sheep.

Bertie's main work was training sheepdogs. He became very well-known as a trainer. Although this didn't earn a fortune, it gained him a lot of respect from the farmers. Derek Cowling would hold sheepdog trials at Rugg's Farm once a year, and Bertie's dog, Lilly, and her partner, Bessy, made him county champion two years running. The litters of these bitches were fetching a good price as hill farmers really need a good sheepdog. As a boy, his father had taught him the trade to be the local pig sticker.

Although the Mill was no longer being used to grind grain, it was saved from total destruction. Bertie and his wife were making a reasonable living in peace and quiet away from the troubles of the war. They had no children at war, although Joyce had a brother who had joined the RAF as a rear gunner with Bomber Command. Joyce and her elder brother, John, were helping by collecting for a Spitfire.

Joyce was a good cook. Her Victoria sponges flew out at the market in Dulverton Town Hall and the Village Hall. They collected £15:2:6d for the War effort. Bertie would take the butter and cream and Joyce's cakes and bread to Minehead Market every other Friday as his contribution. This was an opportunity to socialise with other, more experienced farmers.

Although he had learned a lot from his father in Wales, the Exmoor hill farmers had their own ways. The Mill, being 850 feet above sea level, was not quite on top of the moors, but farming there had a lot in common, mainly being that you could get really bad winters, frost in June and even deep snow at Easter.

(IV)
23 JUNE 1941

Bertie was on the Massey Ferguson that he had borrowed from his brother-in-law. He had just finished turning the hay on this beautiful summer's day and was a little taken aback; there were two MPs questioning Joyce. They looked very threatening! Although he was in a reserved occupation, he didn't like the look of them. As he jumped down from the tractor, he heard them say that they wanted to search the Mill. Bertie had been in a good mood when he arrived, but these men were frightening Joyce. He said to them, 'If you have any problem, talk to me.'

Corporal Morgan was being very officious, but when he heard his Welsh accent, he changed his attitude, and between them, they managed to sort out what this was all about. They were looking for Jerry Winzor, who had joined up, or rather he had enlisted rather than be arrested for his many minor thefts.

Before he had finished his three weeks' basic training in Deal, Jerry had found out that he was not going to be posted to France. So, his plan to follow his dream and desert in France would not work. So, he had gone out on a Friday night pass and never returned. He had managed to dodge the search parties out looking for him and he had discarded his army clothes going from farm to farm at night. As the weather was fine, the farmer's wives left their washing out at night, so he would steal a pair of trousers from one farm and then a shirt from another about three or four miles away so as not to arouse suspicion. He needed to find some shoes, as his army boots would be an immediate giveaway!

He was in luck. In Backhouse Street in Folkestone, a lady was sitting outside buffing up her husband's size ten shoes on a doorstep. She was called away to answer the telephone, and he nonchalantly wandered by and slipped them into his bag and was around the corner before she returned. Just then, a bus had pulled up at a stop, and he had jumped aboard and was away! He went to a dance that night and stole an RAF-issue flying jacket. So, he looked quite well off, and no one would have thought he was an army deserter! He looked for all the world like a fighter pilot.

The next night he found a pub that was full of RAF whalers. He had a wad of money he had found on a farmer's kitchen table, and he joined the pilots and bought them lots of drinks. He managed to get Flying Officer Johnathon Pringle very drunk, and he wagered that he couldn't fly over to France on a night mission and drop a potty full of piss on the Germans in Calais and get back before daylight in one piece. Johnathon said that he would only have a go if Jerry would go with him in the two-seater training Hurricane. They crept up to the Hawkinge Airfield. All was quiet; the RAF police seemed to be having a party.

Jerry and Johnathon found the Hurricane a long way away from the party, and there was no one about it. Johnathon instructed Jerry on how to swing the propeller, and when the engine started, he climbed aboard and discarded the ladder, shutting the cockpit behind him. They taxied into the wind and took off over Capel-le-Ferne. Jerry looked back and could see lots of torches flashing, and then a searchlight swept past them but didn't catch them. By that time, they were out at sea, and they flew above the cloud, so they were lost from sight of the coast. The flight seemed uneventful, and in about half an hour, they were over France. The thing was that Johnathon had been too drunk to think about the fact that the plane had not been refuelled.

CHAPTER 8

Jerry Winzor's Story – Part 2

FRANCE
FORCED LANDING NEAR LE
COLOMBIER

Just as they discovered, they hadn't brought a bucket of piss to bombard the Germans, Johnathon climbed the Hurricane away from Cap Gris-Nez, and the searchlights were switched on. The engine was faltering and spluttering. Johnathon took one look at the fluttering fuel gauge, which was moving towards empty and the truth came in on him! He had been so stupid! While he still had some fuel, he thought about keeping on climbing until the fuel tanks ran dry and trying to glide back across the Channel downhill to the Kent coast, but he would probably be shot down by friendly fire. Jerry had noticed that the fuel was low, but he knew there was enough to get to France, which was his plan, anyway.

He convinced Johnathon to land before they were shot. They glided down silently away from the coast and as far away from habitation as possible. Johnathon made a perfect landing in a field that had just been cut near Le Colombier. It didn't seem as if the Germans had realised they had landed. Jerry left Johnathon with the plane and said he would go and see if he could steal some fuel.

Jerry had no intention of returning with the fuel but he was searching for somewhere to hide away for the night, maybe an isolated barn, but it was a very dark night, and he tripped and fell into a ditch full of very black, smelly, rancid water. The sides of the ditch were very slippery. Every time he nearly reached the top. He lost his footing and slipped back again. He was getting very angry, which didn't help, and he was becoming exhausted! He thought he saw a light flashing, but he couldn't decide whether to call out as he knew he was in enemy territory! The light flashed closer and then across his face.

'*Bonjour! Qui est là?*'

Then a rope fell across his face. It smelled of horse, but what the heck! He grabbed it and started to haul himself up, and suddenly he was at the top of the ditch and face to face with three men.

'*Mercy! Je sui anglais.*'

One of the French farmhands spoke a little English.

'What you do here? You from a plane that landed?'

Jerry had picked up a little French from Eloise, so he managed to say, '*Je cherche du carburant pour l'avion.*' I look for fuel for the plane. Jerry was taken aback when the Frenchman kissed him on both cheeks and gave him a big man hug.

'*Bienvenue en Pas-de Calais!* We must go and get the plane back in the air. *Les allemands le chercheront bientôt.* The Germans will be searching for it soon.'

Jerry didn't really understand, but he got the drift.

They were dowsed by the light as the moon came from behind a cloud and showed them the path to a large barn. They relit their lights when they had closed the heavy oak doors. Jerry couldn't help noticing the crook beams. Hidden behind a pile of what looked like railway sleepers was a stack of fuel cans with British markings. Jerry thought to himself, 'Johnathon, you're in luck.'

He was going to let him take his chances! There was a heavy horse and a very good-looking cart. Without a word, they all set to and loaded and tied down the cargo. The Frenchmen knew where the plane was and very silently went across two fields and unloaded one can of fuel at a time and passed them up onto the wing of the Hurricane, and filled its tanks. They had obviously done this before. Johnathon was making sure that it was all OK. When they had finished, he gave each of the crew a hug and thanked them. He dropped himself into the pilot's seat and waved Jerry to join him in the co-pilot's seat, but Jerry indicated that he was going to stay in France to see 'his woman'.

Johnathon didn't argue. He signalled to the crew to swing the propeller, closed the canopy and as the engine came to mid-revs, Jerry and the crew cleared away from the tail swinging around. He opened the throttles and taxied across the field, and took to the air, just missing the hedge. Before he could reach the cloud base, the searchlight flashed across the fuselage, and the ground-to-air batteries started pumping out flack. All hell, let loose! It looked as if a round had hit and gone straight through the tail, but the damage was small, and before he was hit again, the speed of climb of the Hurricane took Johnathon into the cloud and high enough to be out of range and back to Hawkinge and safety before daylight. He was going to be in big trouble, but it was better than being taken prisoner.

Jerry introduced himself as best he could in franglais as they watched the Hurricane disappear in a hail of bullets.

(II)
THE ANCIENT HOLLOW OAK TREE

The farmers all needed to get back to their homes so that it would appear that they had just woken up when the Germans came to search. So, Jerry had to disappear and hide out for at least two days, maybe more; unless he travelled as far away from the landing site very quickly, he would be in serious trouble. First, the French had a very good place for him to hide. It was a very old oak tree that was so big that it was hollow in the middle at about 2.5 metres above the ground. Very few people knew about this tree as it was in a very difficult place to get to.

It was surrounded by undergrowth and had a really deep ditch all around it, which was a virtual bog in winter and full of brambles. There was only one way to get into it. For some reason, dogs shied away from the tree as if it was haunted. Jerry settled down for the rest of the night. Jean-Paul, who showed him to 'her', had left a blanket, water, wine, and bread there for emergencies. He patted his friendly tree and left him, saying, '*Je m'accorderai quand la côte sera dégagée.*' I will return when the coast is clear.

Jerry woke to the sound of German voices and dogs. He just sat tight, and after a lot of snuffling around and orders being shouted, the sounds faded away. He relaxed and drifted into a fitful sleep for a while. He was woken by shouts in German and then the sound of automatic weapons and the thud of bullets into his hiding place. He knew he had to stay quiet. Things seemed to have changed. Very out of character, Jerry Winzor was worried about Jean-Paul. He had shown him kindness for no apparent reason. For the first time in his life, it seemed that he had a real enemy that was trying to kill his friend! He turned the anger that had been with him since a child into something positive.

(III)
2 JULY 1941

He didn't know what time it was, but it was light, and there were strands of light finding their way through the foliage and into the tree. He sensed that it was about 10 a.m. and decided it was safe to venture out. He had no weapon to defend himself, but it was just as well, as if he had started shooting at the Germans, they would have outgunned him for sure. Best to use a knife, but he had lost the one he had always carried.

When he emerged, all was quiet, but at the bottom of the ancient oak lay the body of his only friend Jean-Paul. He found himself in tears and thought to himself, 'This is really fucking stupid! I've only known the man for five minutes!' Nevertheless, he was very emotional about it. Just as he was about to leave, he heard the trundle of a half-track troop carrier on the road two fields away. He decided that it was not a good idea to go back to his hiding place, so he crossed into the next field away from the road. He found a lane that didn't look as if it had been used for ages. There were hoof marks in the mud, so he carefully tried to walk in these so as to cover his tracks.

The lane led to a disused barn attached to a farmhouse. He didn't think he could stay there for long, but for the moment, it was just what he needed. He would wait there till dark and then find some food. Later, while out scavenging for food, he overheard a French conversation between the farmer and his wife. It seemed to be about things like 'eggs'. He did understand a little and what he didn't understand he gathered from the intonation of the conversation.

He moved closer to try to hear better and his foot went through a rotten board, and there was a terrible squawking as he landed on a hen's nesting box. There were broken eggs, feathers and chickens running around. The cockerel, defending his brood, was not best pleased with Jerry. Flapping his wings, he attacked him, pecking at his ear and nose, drawing blood. Jerry managed to stand, covered in straw, egg whites, yokes, and shells, just as the farmer, whom he recognised, came in with his shotgun to kill the supposed fox. Monsieur Phillipe couldn't help but burst into laughter. Out of character, they both sat down in fits of laughter.

But there was nothing to laugh about as the German soldiers were searching for the house, and they came out to see what all the fuss was about. They looked in the barn and started to laugh as well. This broke the tension of a serious search. They didn't even think that Jerry was other than a local! They just boarded their transport and left. Philippe couldn't believe his and Jerry's luck. The next move would have been the Gestapo, torture and maybe death for the whole family. Philippe had recognised Jerry under all that egg and straw, and Jerry told Philippe about Jean-Paul and said that he would, in some way or other, take revenge.

Philippe said in broken franglais that there would be a lot of revenge, especially for the traitors to France, the supporters of *'ce salaud* Pétain working for the Nazis'. They both went to find Jean-Paul. As the dead man had lived as a hermit, no one could remember when he arrived in the village or where he came from. He did have a local accent. He was loved by all the village. He used to ride his rusty old bicycle from his place in the oak tree where he had lived for many years. Then a tumble-down cottage was put together by the villagers for him for the winter. Most of the time, he had preferred to stay in the oak tree. Jerry was upset and emotional about his only friend's death. He really needed to get away from Le Colombier, but he was going to have to take the chance that he might be picked up by the Germans.

They didn't have a service in the church, but the local priest, Frère Jerome, came to the oak, and he was buried there at the foot of the tree that had protected him for all those years!

Afterwards, Philippe and the baptist found Jerry some very French-looking clothes, French bread, cider, and wine. They said Jean-Paul wouldn't want his old bicycle, so he might as well take it. Jerry gave them the sheepskin flying jacket (they would have to hide as it was rather a giveaway). It could be traded for a lot of money. He stayed the night and had food with trusted villagers. They taught him some local French phases and said if he acted as if he was simple and didn't wash so he smelt, the Germans might tease him, but they would probably leave him alone. They were fairly green troops. They hadn't caught on to this deception yet.

(IV)
15 JULY 1941

Jerry Winzor, on his very old rusty bicycle, stayed away from main roads and found old farm tracks as much as he could. The bicycle was so rickety that he was not getting very far on his epic journey, and he didn't even have a map! He was heading more or less south and slightly east. He didn't know exactly where Eloise's parents lived, but he knew it was fairly close to the Pyrenees. She had mentioned a town or city called Pau.

When Eloise had left the Mill in a great hurry, she had left a lot of stuff behind. Among these things was a faded photo of the farm, her mother, father, brother and younger sister, near the entrance gate of the farm. There was a very old sign with the name on it, but it was very hard to read. Jerry had brought this and some of Eloise's clothes and underwear, which reminded him of her smell. It kept this dream of finding her and her falling in love with him alive. He had taken so many chances and really needed to have this dream to keep him going. In his heart, he knew that she would be frightened of him after their last encounter. But since then, he had changed! He was trying to come to terms with this; he felt that it would make him weak. He didn't know what was to come next.

War brings out the worst and the best in ordinary people. He didn't consider himself ordinary. Along the way, he would find remote farms and barns to sleep in. Farmer's wives treated him as a tramp and gave him food and cider or wine. He pretended that he was dumb. As he was very dirty (he hadn't washed or shaved for days) and was riding on a very old French bicycle, he fitted this image very well. If he heard a truck in the distance, he would hide. His luck and good judgement held for many kilometres. He just didn't know where he was! He felt he was going in the right direction, but he needed to get a map. There was no way he could ask for directions!

(V)
SMALL TOWN OF SAINTE-GEMMES-SUR-LOIRE
19 JULY

He left it till nightfall and then broke into the library. There was a German post in the town. Many of the senior officers had taken over the attractive houses on the banks of the Loire, so Jerry had to be very careful not to arouse the drowsy guards at the Hôtel de Ville. He was not a stranger to breaking and entering. He found a small window on the ground floor and managed to prise the window open with a jemmy he had purloined from a shed nearby. He didn't want to turn on any lights, but very conveniently, there had been a lot of power cuts, and the librarians had prepared oil lights so they could keep working if the power failed. Jerry had a Zippo lighter he had won from an American in a card game. He took the oil lamp into a windowless room and was able to light his way to find a decent map. The only one was in a frame in the lobby. He removed it from the frame and folded it. Luckily all the shutters had been closed in case of bombing, so he made his escape through the same window he had entered. But just as he jumped down, a dog started to bark! With the oil lamp and the map, he made a run for it into the woods on the edge of the village. But now he was being followed by German soldiers who had been aroused by the dog barking.

Jerry thought quickly, and as he entered the woodland, he hid the map and his bag in a bush. The soldiers were catching up with him, and he knew that if he kept running, they wouldn't give up. He decided that if he just gave himself up before they started shooting, he would use his acting ability to make them think he was just a simple dumb tramp looking for somewhere to get his head down.

They caught up with him. As the lights flashed past him, he put up his hands. They didn't look further. They just frog-marched him to the office and cuffed him to a chair. Again, his luck held, as these Germans were not very bright and as the Obergefreiter in charge was asleep, they decided not to wake him as this was a civil matter. So they just put Jerry in a cell; they would tell the town gendarme in the morning.

At 7 a.m., the guard changed and Valentin, the town gendarme, tried to interrogate Jerry, but he couldn't get any sense out of him, so he took him to the police station. Jerry took a big risk and communicated that he was a sympathiser with the Resistance. At first, he thought he had made a mistake!

He was marched out and into the French police Citroën van and driven off. This was all for show; when they came to a farm a kilometre down a hidden track out of town, Valentin introduced him to the farmer, who said in broken franglais he was hiding an RAF pilot. They thought that Jerry was there to help get him back to England. Jerry played along with this as he was trying to get to the Pyrenees in the free zone. This went down well with the Resistance as they had contacts all through the zone to the Spanish border. He didn't need the map, but he did need his bag. It wasn't wise for him to go into town, so he told one of the locals where he had left it, and soon Marian had returned on her bicycle, with his bag under her shopping. Peter (the flying officer) and Jerry had supper.

After dark, they set off south-east following the route they had been given. There was a rusty old van left for them about 7 km away in a deserted barn, which was on a track going towards Poitiers, near the border with the free zone. They travelled in the very early morning or evening (the light on the van didn't work all the time) and at twilight when the German (rather green troops) were having their evening meal. As this was just the beginning of the Nazi occupation, they thought that the

French country folk were all ignorant peasants. Peter spent most of the time in the back of the van as he would stand out like a sore thumb. They kept to tracks, and stayed the night in old sheds, and continued following the route they were given. The organisation was good, as very often they found that food and wine, or cider had been left for them.

As they came closer to the free zone border, there seemed to be an intensification of Nazi troops, so they dumped the van and walked through woodland and alongside small streams, thus avoiding the concentration of villages and towns for four nights.

(VI)
22 JULY

At first, they didn't realise that they had crossed into the free zone. They had lost their way but were going southeast at night with very little moonlight, but they came to a river and followed it till they came to a barn.

It didn't seem to be occupied, but they could hear sounds coming from inside. Jerry very cautiously edged up to the door where there was a chink of light showing. Then the door suddenly opened and knocked him flat on his back. A car came out at speed without lights and was gone. A couple of men followed it and went to close the door before Jerry had time to recover and make his escape. They picked him up off the floor and held him at gunpoint. He hadn't had time to warn Peter, who was following Jerry at a distance.

The men dragged both of them into the barn and tied them to a very large oak post. Their captors hadn't yet said a word, and neither Peter nor Jerry dared say anything; they had no idea if they were friends or foes.

At last, one of the locally dressed men said something in what seemed to be a local French accent. '*Qui es-tu?!!*' The biggest fellow kneed Peter in the crotch!

Peter crumpled, and Jerry shouted, '*Cessez!* Stop!' The other was about to hit Jerry again when he realised that he had said stop in English.

'*Tu es anglais?*'

Jerry tried to explain, but they didn't understand. Eventually, after an argument, Peter recovered and used his schoolboy French to try to explain. The farmers seemed to understand, relented, and released them. Peter, still holding his parts in pain, said he was a Spitfire pilot. At last, they understood! They changed from violence to man hugs, kisses on both cheeks, and handshakes. 'Come, come!' they beckoned, and they were led to the edge of a riverbank.

(VII)
THE RIVER VIENNE '(ICI LA VIENNE')

There was a small boat alongside the bank, and all four boarded, and silently they were punted upriver. There was a wooded bank, and the locals steered into the shallows beneath the trees. They had heard the rumble of an engine and hid out of the way until a German patrol boat passed by! The river was a good way to travel as the patrols were very limited. The Germans had very few riverboats, and you could hear them coming from a long way off. Jean-Philippe punted on, keeping close to the riverbank, as the current was strong and they were going upstream.

They reached a very small, flooded ditch that was hidden by overgrowth. After about 200 metres, it began to widen out and became easy to negotiate. Behind a large clump of willows, there was what looked like an abandoned house. This was an excellent hiding place! Only a few locals, probably fishermen, would know it was there. Jean-Philippe and the man, who hadn't said a word, tied the boat up and helped Peter and Jerry onto the hidden stage. They all climbed ashore, and Jean-Philippe opened a door hidden by hanging plants that looked like a very old grapevine. They entered into a large kitchen with a log fire, on which stood a steaming cauldron. Around the large old kitchen table, several other men sat as a farmer's wife doled out the broth from the cauldron. There was the smell of fresh baked bread.

Neither Peter nor Jerry had eaten for days; they were starving! Their tongues were almost hanging out as they introduced themselves by going around the table and shaking hands with everyone. Room was made for them to sit down, and they were given fresh bread and chabròl. Then the wine bag was handed around, so everyone had a swig. When Peter's turn came, he spilt more than he drank. Jerry managed a bit better. It took both of them a while to get the hang of it. Jerry thought that it was only the Spanish who drank from a wine bag! Then he realised that some of the people around the table were from the Pyrenees. This was great as that was the direction both the Englishmen were going. After the serious business of food came the business of war on the Germans.

One of the groups, who identified himself as Joseph, spoke English, and he was not very happy that Jean-Philippe had brought this Englishman there. If they were captured, they might give it away to the Nazis.

'We need to get you as far away from here as possible,' he relayed in French to the others.

Jerry said to Joseph that he was heading for a safe place in Pau. It was a lie, but he needed to have some sort of explanation.

'Peter needs to get across the Pyrenees and back to the UK so he can bomb the shit out of them! I'm working for the Resistance.'

He expected approval, but there was a lack of enthusiasm, although the story did seem to satisfy them. Jerry and Peter didn't understand much of what was being discussed, but they picked up enough to realise that they were planning a big offensive against the Germans. From the bits of French that Peter understood, they were going to blow up a train with weapons for the Spanish government. They were going to wait until the train got to the Pyrenees. This would disable any tracks in the mountains. Best that it was done in a tunnel so that it would take a very long time to rebuild. They felt that it was best to let the train get into the Somport Tunnel.

Jerry was up for helping them. He managed to put his oar into the discussion, communicating with Joseph that he had had training in explosives in the army, again bullshit, but they believed him. His only experience had been with fireworks on bonfire night! He was really keen to be recognised in the Resistance. The company was just about to break up when there was a loud banging as the door was knocked down. Then five German soldiers with automatic weapons forced their way in through the door. However, the soldiers hadn't realised that they had been followed by the lookouts, who knifed three of them in the back! Joseph and Jean-Philippe produced guns and shot the other two. But this place was compromised, and they had to dispose of the bodies and vacate! Peter and Jerry were really shocked by all this! Neither of them had really had such a near-death experience before.

They found the patrol boat tied up at the staging, and loaded the bodies of the soldiers. They disabled the radio, and the whole company boarded. They moved the patrol boat further up the stream away from the main river. About a mile on through the overgrown steam, there was a tumble-down boat shed. They hid the patrol boat there for about three hours. In the dead of night, they moved it with the weighted bodies in it and sank it in the deepest part of La Vienne. By the time the Nazis had worked out what had happened, the group had dispersed to meet up again three days later near Pau.

(VIII)
23 JULY 1941

Jerry Winzor and Peter (Jerry never knew his surname) were given some directions to follow the river south and east as much as possible, keeping away from large towns. They would go from farm to farm as there was always a friendly farmer's wife or an open kitchen door with bread and eggs to steal. It was going to take them a lot longer than three days.

They came to a dilapidated farm shed that looked to be a good place to get their heads down. It was getting dark on the third day of their journey, and they were getting hungry.

They hadn't had any luck. The village was Valence-sur-Baïse. The local *tabac* was open, so Jerry (looking very local) decided that he could get a drink and maybe find some food. As he entered, he realised that he had done the wrong thing, but he couldn't turn around and leave, as the German soldiers at the bar would smell a rat! He had to use his acting ability to get out of this one. He sat down at a table in a dark corner. He realised that the Germans were too busy getting drunk to take any notice of him, and he mimed to the barman that he was dumb. He wasn't stupid.

He picked up a bottle of absinthe and a glass and set up a drink for Jerry as if he was a local who did this every day. Then the barman returned to pour more drinks at the bar.

Jerry wanted to leave, but he was hoping that the soldiers would leave first. He thought the best thing to do was be very brazen, so he walked up to the bar and slapped a coin on the bar in payment and walked out before they realised what had happened. It very nearly worked, but a drunken Nazi soldier can be dangerous. One of them tripped Jerry up on purpose and started to kick him for no apparent reason. They all laughed and started to have a go at him. Much against his instincts, he just lay there until the barman came to help him up.

The Nazis had their fun and upped and left without paying for their drinks. Maurice, the barman, chased after them, but they abused him in German and fell about laughing.

Jerry got up, and as Maurice returned, he realised that Jerry wasn't French and was probably on the escape route to the Pyrenees. Jerry's luck was still holding! Maurice helped him into the backroom. He spoke to him in what little English he had, and he said that he had been primed by the Resistance. He knew Joseph, who had been there a day ago. Jerry tried to explain that he needed to take some food and drink to Peter, who was hidden in a barn outside the village. Maurice just ushered him out of the back door, and Jerry pointed the way to the hiding place.

They made their way through back gardens away from the main street. It was just as well that they had left the *tabac*, as a half-track troop carrier arrived in the village square and a dozen soldiers jumped out and crouched down in positions around the square. Then a Mercedes staff car with two very senior and highly decorated German officers swung into the square followed by a truck with 20 soldiers in it stopped briefly on the road to Auch. The soldiers all reboarded the troop carrier and the truck and disappeared in a cloud of dust. Maurice really thought that they had come to arrest him and shut down his place. He breathed a sigh of relief. They went through the back door of his house into the kitchen. His wife was cooking some fish for supper.

Jerry made his way to the hiding place saying, 'Come on, Peter, we're in for a treat – a cooked supper.'

Peter, 'What's on the menu?'

'Fresh fish,' was Jerry's reply.

On the way, Jerry gave an outline of what had happened. Peter had heard the trucks and the roar as they left so stayed put until Jerry arrived. It was getting dark, so they could move more freely. Peter said that he was very lucky to have Jerry as a companion.

Jerry said, 'I wouldn't have survived five minutes on my own. I've been a loner all my life. It made me streetwise. I just take life as it comes. I don't expect anything from anyone. I just get the best I can at that moment! It seems that in war, that is your best defence. I have nothing to lose except my life, and up to now, it hasn't been worth much.'

Somehow war can bring out the best and the worst in people. Jerry had been the worst, and war had brought out his best. He felt that he had been saved by the suffering of others. He had the training as a criminal to use against a lawless, ruthless enemy that was destroying all the very bases of the life that he had fought against, but when he saw it being destroyed, he found its value.

This seemed to be a sort of quiet moment to savour as they ate and chatted, half in French and half in English. They drank some wine and ate the best French meal they'd had in a long time. This interlude was short-lived, but it made it possible for them to keep going. Tomorrow was another day!

After thanking Maurice and Anna and exchanging hugs and kisses, they left to sleep in the barn. Who knew what the following day would bring?

(IX)
ON THE ROAD TO A MEETING IN CHÂTEAU DE CUQUERON

Château de Cuqueron

Jerry Winzor found a baker's bicycle in a ditch, and they took turns peddling or riding in the front basket. This was very uncomfortable as they had to keep off the main roads and use farm tracks. Their progress was very slow, but they were trying to find their way to the Château du Cuqueron. However, they were making good progress and found one of the old farm buildings near Lembeye that Joseph had told them about. It didn't seem close to any farms and was a safe place to stay overnight.

There was a very dirty-looking rusty cupboard leaning against the cob wall. They couldn't believe it as Peter opened it; he just managed to catch the bread and wine stashed in it.

Just as they sat on some hay bales to eat, the rickety double doors creaked open! They both reacted by falling back behind the bales, spilling their food and drink. Jerry pulled a pistol from his pocket and was just about to shoot when he recognised Patrick. He was one of the group who had shot the Germans on the Vienne river. He had brought some cheese and cider. He didn't speak a lot of English, but they managed to have a good laugh! The wine and cider certainly helped. Patrick said in his broken English that he had seen them arrive on the baker's bicycle when at the barn they had hit a pothole and fallen in a heap!

They had decided to dump the bike and walk. Peter had become very cheesed off as he seemed to be riding in the basket most of the time. The problem was that it was years since he had ridden a bicycle. And he wasn't doing very well at pushing the pedals.

Patrick had his open pickup truck hidden behind the barn, which was full of vegetables to take to the Saturday market the following day in Monein, very close to Château de Cuqueron.

All three fell asleep after a lot of wine. When a cockerel crowed at 5 a.m., it seemed like the middle of the night. They woke feeling very under the weather but managed to climb in the back of the truck and hide themselves among the wooden boxes.

Peter was a bit worried about Patrick's driving, and to begin with, he was justified. It was lucky there was very little traffic, and by the time they reached the main road, Patrick had managed to drive in a straight line. Jerry said, 'If you can't do anything about it, relax!!' Although the ride was not very comfortable, they both nodded off, more in a drunken stupor than anything else.

Before they reached the market town, Patrick turned off to find the château. It was just as well as about 2 km closer to Monein there was a French gendarme and German-run roadblock checking all the vehicles as they entered the town. Peter and Jerry were pleased to arrive. Patrick must have been used to getting drunk and going to the market the next morning. He just helped them down and drove off to set up his stall, but there he was, searched at the roadblock. Luckily, there was no problem.

They were a day early, and the place appeared to be deserted. There was a tap in the stable yard, and before doing anything else, they washed themselves and drank a lot of water and sat in the sun.

They were rudely awoken by the sound of vehicles arriving, so they hid in a hayloft in the nearest stable. They had a view of the yard through a crack in the half-door. It seemed to be the local gendarmerie accompanied by two senior German officers in their Mercedes. They banged on the front doors. There was no answer, so they came round to the kitchen door next to the stables.

Eventually, little old Madame Adele appeared. They pushed her aside. Jerry didn't think they suspected anything. It looked as if they were just viewing prospective lodgings for officers of the occupying army. They didn't stay long. Peter managed to pick up enough words in French to work out that the advance party felt that the château was not up to the standard that a general would expect.

Jerry and Peter stayed put for a couple of hours until more vehicles arrived, which drove straight into the stable yard. This time they recognised one or two of the occupants and so they came down from their hiding place to tell what had just occurred.

Jean-Baptiste seemed to be the leader. He said that was great as it meant that they had checked it out and were unlikely to return in the near future. Jerry suddenly realised that Jean-Baptiste spoke perfect English, which was a shock. They were ushered into the kitchen, and the whole party sat around the enormous pine table. They all seemed very relaxed as Jean-Baptiste introduced himself and the other four: Patrick, whom they knew; Henry, a rangy, very tall fellow, who had a moody threatening presence; Gabriel, who smiled all the time (Jerry didn't trust him); and Daniel who was laid back and friendly.

THE AUCTION ROOM

They were just settling down to drinking when the door creaked open and a very attractive woman in her forties walked in. Jerry couldn't believe his eyes!

It was Eloise. She didn't seem to have recognised him, and he tried to hide himself; it had really taken him off balance. He had previously worked out the way he was going to approach her when he finally met her, but this certainly wasn't what he had planned!

Eloise seemed to be in charge of this group and sat down at the top of the table and organised Adele, the elderly housekeeper.

'Nous devons faire des affaires importantes. Nous ferions mieux de nourrir cette racaille avant qu'ils ne deviennent trop ivres.' We need to do some important business. We had better feed this rabble before they get too drunk. Who are these two? I've not seen them before!' Jean-Baptiste explained, and as Eloise spoke English, she started interrogating Peter.

He said he was Flying Officer Peter Franklin. 'I parachuted from my Hurricane some weeks ago near Valence and am trying to get back home.'

Eloise was satisfied with that and ignored Jerry, who breathed a sigh of relief. He just didn't know how to deal with this; it wasn't in his comfort zone. In the past, he would have used his ego to blast his way through. This had deserted him; he just kept a low profile, hoping he could find a way of solving his predicament.

She took a detailed map of the Pyrenees from a drawer in the table and unrolled it for all to see. They discussed the best place to derail the train in order to cause the most disruption. Jean-Baptiste reckoned that the best place would be in a tunnel. Eloise realised that it was too close to her heart. They were planning to blow up a train on the very same line where the drama that her beloved Frank had been the hero in 1915. She couldn't deal with this at first, but she went along with Jean-Baptiste until she suddenly stood up and left the room. She couldn't let them see her in tears!

Jerry saw this as an opportunity to comfort his imagined love! This was a way to build bridges. He followed her out to the passage where she was sobbing silently in a corner. Jerry touched her on the shoulder, and she whipped around and slapped him across the face.

'Qu'est-ce que tu fais ici! Toi, bâtard, je ne veux pas te voir; vous devriez être arrêté.' What are you doing here! You bastard, I don't want to see you; you should be arrested!

Jerry recovered quickly. He hadn't expected a welcome, but he hadn't thought that Eloise had recognised him either. His dream had been shattered, and he nearly turned back to his former arrogant self. Something stopped him; he had left that shoddy character behind where his only friend who had saved his life had been shot by the oak tree.

By this stage, Eloise had pulled herself together just as Jean-Baptiste came to see what the fuss was about. They left Jerry licking his wounds in the hallway and recommenced their planning. Peter, who had been trained in live ammunition and explosives, was able to give some useful tips in schoolboy French and franglais. Decisions had to be made quickly, but the first thing was food and wine.

THE AUCTION ROOM

By the time Jerry had recovered, they had eaten, and it was getting dark, so the meeting broke up, but the group left one by one, in or on different modes of transport, and all in different directions. Eloise left with Patrick in a battered Renault but went over the fields. Peter was taken by Henry in his 2CV but not on the roads, on tracks and through dried-up streams. They were heading to the barn in the deserted farm next to Eloise's father's farm, at Saint-Jean-de-Luz, and then on to Saint-Girons and the beginning of the trek over the Pyrenees and back to Kent.

For a while, Jerry thought he had been left to be captured by the gendarmes, but Jean-Baptiste came up behind him with a gun in his back. 'You tried to rape Eloise 20 years ago! What are you doing here now?'

Jerry turned, ignoring the gun.

'That was the old Jerry Winzor. I've come to find Eloise and try to make it up to her. She lost her love, Frank, 20 years ago. He was my undoing. I was a bitter man over a childish fight. I have found the real enemy, the Nazis, who killed my only friend Jean-Paul, who saved my life in Le Colombier. Just let me help you in the Resistance. I have no life in England. I can't return as I am a deserter. I'm a loner; I have to fight my own fights. My life has not been worth much. So, if I die in this private war, I want it to be for something!'

Jean-Baptiste was taken aback by this outburst of passion. He just gave Jerry a man hug and they left together.

Little did they know it, but they were just in time; against expectations, in the morning, the general's entourage came back to take over the château.

(X)
ELOISE PESTONE'S PARENTS' FARM AT BUZIET, NEAR ARUDY

Eloise returned home to find her sister, Sarah, and her husband, Pierre, sitting at the table and her father asleep in front of the fire in his favourite chair, which Frank had made for his grandfather as a present. It was lunchtime, and Sarah had made a meal, which was in the oven.

Pierre was a distant relation, third or fourth cousin. Eloise didn't get on with that side of the family, but her sister was married to him, so she had to be civil to him.

Since their mother had died six years before, her father had become sullen. He was still in mourning for his beloved wife. Eloise had become the head of the family. She was a disappointment to her father as she hadn't married. But she had produced a grandson for him.

Francis had just finished turning the hay. He came in stripped to the waist. He had a wash down and was ready for a meal. He put on a shirt as a respect for his mother and sat down at the table to eat. Eloise woke her father and helped him to the table. He was being very moody and turned on Pierre because he was sitting in his chair.

Pierre said to Sarah, 'I think we should be going! He doesn't appreciate what you do for him!'

Francis was unhappy that his grandfather was so bad-tempered. He loved his aunt and wanted them to get on, but Pierre was very caustic and somehow promoted the historic bad feeling between the families. They left to go home to their family farm 5 km away.

As they ate, Eloise recounted how Jerry Winzor was working with the Resistance. She said she couldn't understand how or why he was there. Eloise said that she was frightened of him and didn't want him anywhere near her. Francis, who had taken an instant dislike to Jerry 20 years ago in Brompton, became very protective of his mother and said, 'I'll sort him out!'

The next day Francis met up with Patrick, and they cooked up a way of getting rid of Jerry. They sent a message to bring him to a cave for a planning meeting. 'Leave him there on his own overnight.'

Francis told his Uncle Pierre that there was an escaped prisoner hiding there. Francis knew that Pierre's brother-in-law was a gendarme and Nazi sympathiser. Pierre couldn't keep his mouth shut! This information would get through very quickly.

That night Jean-Baptiste arrived at Saint-Jean-de-Luz and told Eloise what Jerry had said. She would not accept it and didn't believe that he could change. Francis came in from work and told his mother that he had sorted Jerry and that the Pétains would either lock him up or turn him over to the Gestapo.

Both Eloise and Jean-Baptiste were appalled and angry that Francis had done this. It was very stupid of him, because if the Gestapo got hold of Jerry, he could give away a lot of the Resistance safe houses. And Jean-Baptiste believed in Jerry's change of heart. Also, the cave was a very good 'safe place'. He and Eloise decided that the posse of gendarmes and German soldiers would never get to the cave and must be diverted.

So, they organised a rock fall. This would happen when the posse was on a very narrow ledge with a sheer 200-metre drop on one side. It was unlikely that they could survive this. Just in case, Eloise and Patrick would shoot any survivors. As it happened, there was a sudden change in the weather in the morning. The posse was on their way in torrential rain. As they reached the narrow ledge, a waterfall of rocks happened naturally. There was one survivor and he was just looking for shelter and entered the cave, and Jerry shot him dead and pushed him to join his compatriots.

Eloise didn't want to allow Jerry back into her life, but it seemed she had no choice. The only hiding place was the cave where Frank and she had stayed on their first night of love. She took him there, and there seemed an inevitability about this that neither of them could fight.

Jean-Baptiste took some bread and wine and started out to visit Jerry and found them sitting and talking in English. He joined them as he was slightly worried that her lightning temper might erupt. They seemed to be on very civil terms. There was a lot for them to sort out, so he left them to it. He wasn't worried about Eloise as much as Jerry, but all seemed to be calm.

Jerry told Eloise how he had deserted and managed to get a lift in a Hurricane, and his only thought was to get to see her. He said that it was a foolish dream that they could get together. This had sustained him through danger after danger. So, he had managed to fulfil this part, but he expected that she would kick him in the balls and tell the Gestapo, who would likely torture him. Eloise said this had nearly happened as Francis was understandably being very protective of his mother. She said that Jerry couldn't come to the farmhouse as her brother-in-law was friendly with a sympathiser. And her sister and Pierre didn't know that she was a big wheel in the local Resistance. She thought that all the men that visited her were trying to get off with her. Eloise had kept this up as it was a good cover. Even Francis suspected but didn't know anything about her activities with the Resistance. It was best not to know. There were very few people she could trust. The Vichy had spies everywhere. Her neighbours thought she was a slut, 'that unmarried mother who came back from England with a baby'.

Francis suspected something, but he loved and trusted his mother and knew better than to ask. He just kept his head down and ran the farm for his grandfather. This war divided families and friends. But he was still very angry about Jerry. He had heard that the posse that was going to capture him had been killed by a natural rock fall and that the bodies had been washed away across the Spanish border. So, the gendarme could not investigate what had happened. The German commander in Pau was asked to investigate, but they felt that it was a local issue and could not waste their valuable time on it. But Francis was not satisfied, so he decided he would see if he could find Jerry and deliver him up to the authorities! For the moment, he was busy on the farm.

Jean-Baptiste came back to the farm, asking if he had seen Eloise. This was a cover because he didn't want to tell Francis that Jerry and Eloise seemed to have made up their differences. Jean-Baptiste had a respect that bordered on love for Eloise. This seemed to be how she could command the Resistance group. Without realising it, Jean-Baptiste had dropped a hint that Jerry was at the cave where Eloise and Frank had consummated their relationship and probably where Francis was conceived. Francis took note of this and decided that he would go and confront Jerry. What he didn't know was that Eloise was already there!

THE AUCTION ROOM

(XI)
THE CAVE NEAR DE LYS, NOUVELLE-AQUITAINE

Jerry and Eloise had sat and talked. They seemed to be drawn to each other by a force neither of them understood!

Eloise felt that she should have shot him dead on sight, but they were fatally attracted to each other. It was partly sex, as neither of them had had a sexual encounter in years. Eloise had had plenty of offers as she had developed into a very attractive 40-year-old woman. She was endowed with large breasts, and she had kept herself slim through hard work and exercise on the farm. She didn't show her breasts off because she was not looking for a partner! But nevertheless, she used her good looks as a tool to give her status in the area.

Jerry had used *his* charisma and good looks to *his* advantage. He had very high sexual energy that he had converted into his ability to move very quickly, change tack and dodge dangers. Since the age of 14, he had always been able to get away with using his charm to get what he wanted, particularly with the opposite sex. It seemed that Eloise was his endgame. He had been rejected by her. He couldn't understand how his energy had not overcome her. He had always been in charge! This had the effect of him giving in to his emotions. Now he just wanted to love her.

Eloise stood up saying, 'You must stay here until we meet to do the job.'

Jerry went to just shake her hand. But Eloise took his hand and put it to her breast and pulled him violently to her. Jerry hesitated as he wasn't used to a woman making the first move, but he just wanted to feel the warmth of her body against him. This overcame any defence. She pushed him to the ground and lifted her skirt, and sat on his face. While he was still in shock, she turned around and ripped his shirt off and slid her hand down into his trousers and into his crotch as she undid his belt with the other hand. She opened his fly and took hold of his member. Jerry had recovered and was burying his face in her, and brought his hand up. Buttons flew as he opened her shirt and lifted her pendulous breasts. Blindly, he felt for her nipples and pulled them both at the same time, suckling her and bringing her close to a climax. She leaned forward so her nipples were dragging across this member and then cupped his balls. She allowed his member into her mouth. They both climaxed at the same time, and Eloise relaxed and rolled over onto the ground.

Jerry didn't know what had hit him. They both realised that this had been inevitable. They had needed this to happen, but they both realised that it was not the same as Frank and Eloise's relationship. Eloise had taken control and had released Jerry from his unrealistic dream of love and a future with her.

They were just readjusting their dress when they heard some stones falling off the path and dropping into the valley. They hid behind a boulder in the cave, and Eloise said, 'What are you doing here, Francis?'

THE AUCTION ROOM

Before another word was said, Francis had shot Jerry. The bullet had caught hit him low in his calf. He crumpled to the ground in pain. Eloise was behind him and went to help him, and Francis fired a reflex shot that hit his mother in the chest. She fell on top of Jerry!

Francis realised what he had done, dropped the gun and ran to his mother to help her. It was too late. She was already dead. He rolled Eloise off Jerry and tried to resuscitate her, but it was no good; she had gone. Jerry recovered from the shock and pain, and his first reaction was to knock Francis away from her and see if there was any sign of life. He could only confirm that she had left this world.

Francis was in a terrible state and tried to bring his mother back to life. He was crying and putting his arms around her, lifting her, trying to breathe life into the woman who had brought him into this world. He turned on Jerry and flung a wild punch at him, and screamed, 'It's all your fault!'

Jerry put his arms around him in a bear hug, and they both sobbed in emotional regret. They knew there was nothing they could do. Jerry's pain from his leg was secondary to his grief. They just stayed in an embrace, trying to understand how this could have happened to the woman they both loved. They stayed there for what seemed like hours. Neither of them knew what to do to stem the pain of their loss.

Francis disengaged and reached for the gun to shoot himself! The realisation of what he had done was just too much for him. Jerry managed to take the gun from Francis and put his arms around him again. He threw the gun behind a rock and out of Francis's sight. Francis was inconsolable and collapsed in uncontrolled sobs.

'*Comment puis-je vivre sans ma belle mère?* How can I live without my beautiful mother? *Elle était mon rocher!* She was my rock! *Que vais-je faire sans elle?* What am I going to do without her?'

Jerry could not find any words that would stem the flow of grief. He knew that he was the source and the essence of the events that had led to this moment. If it had not been for his arrogant attempt to rape Eloise all those years ago, she would not have died this way. He couldn't do anything about the past. He determined that, if Francis would let him, he would try to help him through this terrible time. They both collapsed in separate grief and pain.

Jean-Baptiste arrived. He could not believe the sight of devastation; it was overwhelming. These were his friends, Francis and Jerry, holding on to each other. Eloise, the woman he had followed, loved, and admired, her life in a river of blood draining over the edge of the precipice.

Death was commonplace in war. But this wasn't part of that. It was a personal tragedy that should not have happened. At first, he was at a loss to know how to deal with it. He prised the two of them apart and took Francis, still sobbing, in his arms and tried to comfort him, but Francis just tried again to kill himself by pulling away to throw himself over the edge to join his mother's lifeblood.

Jean-Baptiste pulled him back. '*Ta mère ne voudrait pas' que tu fasses ça. ... Elle voudrait que tu vives et que tu l'aimes!'* Your mother wouldn't have wanted you to do that. She would have wanted you to live and love her!'

With that, Francis collapsed.

Jerry limped over to help Jean-Baptiste pull Francis well away from the edge and behind the boulder at the back of the cave. He picked up the gun so that Francis wouldn't try it again. He realised that Francis had meant to kill Jerry and that it had all gone terribly wrong. He decided he must dress Jerry's leg. It looked as if, as usual, his luck had held. The bullet had passed through his flesh and just scraped his bone. Jean-Baptiste ripped the bottom of Eloise's skirt and bound the wound to stop the flow of blood.

Then they had to get both Francis and Eloise back to the farm. There was a problem as they could not allow this incident to become public. Eloise wouldn't have wanted that. There were too many Vichy spies around, and this would certainly put into doubt the operation to blow up the train. It could also expose the Resistance group and have very serious consequences for the organisation, the escape route, and other people on the edges of these groups.

Jean-Baptiste talked to Jerry about the way forward. They agreed that they must find a way out of this to make it seem like a shooting accident, which, in fact, it was. But they would have to keep Jerry out of it. Jean-Baptiste gave directions to Jerry to another safe house that was deserted, for him to hide out in until he had organised moving Eloise from the cave and setting up a fictional scenario for Sarah, her sister, and the gendarme, who would have to be informed.

Sarah was going to be devastated, and she would want to know all the details, but because of Pierre, her husband, there must not be any suspicion that this had anything to do with Jerry or the Resistance. He had to leave Eloise in the cave and find Patrick. What to do about Francis? He couldn't be left with Eloise as he was liable to jump off the edge. They decided that he would have to go with Jerry. This was not going to be easy as he was in such an emotional state. He would not just walk with the man whom he blamed for the death of his mother. Jean-Baptiste decided that he had to be drugged or drunk and then carried away from the cave. They were feeding him with that brandy that he always had with him.

In the nick of time, Patrick appeared at the entrance to the cave. Visibly shocked at the vision before him, he put two and two together very quickly! He didn't quite know what had happened, but he realised that they would have to take Eloise and Francis away from there. He knew that Francis was after Jerry's blood. He had come here to sort him out. He didn't expect to find Eloise dead! He agreed with Jean-Baptiste that this had to look like an accident, but not there. First, they had to carry Eloise down near the river in the valley, and second, Francis had to be hidden until the next day. He was getting very drunk, but they wanted him to pass out! They needed time to convince Sarah, but they couldn't tell her about the cave.

They stretched a coat over two branches to make a stretcher, and made a pulley with a log, and cranked it down into the valley by the river. Jerry half carried and walked the drunken Francis down. Patrick had arranged a meeting with Henry, Gabriel, and Daniel in another safe house.

He ran off to find them to get their help and returned an hour later. The five of them decided that the best thing to do would be for Jerry and Francis to take the escape route to England. They would be taken to Saint-Girons, the start of the escape route over the Pyrenees.

(XII)
ELOISE'S PARENTS' FARM AT BUZIET NEAR ARUDY

Monsieur Pestone was quite lazy. Being the *maire*, he was expected to do a lot of administrative work and read papers that the village had sent him, but it ended up with his assistant doing much of this work. He was spending most of his time snoozing and reading and occasionally signing stuff. Sarah was a good daughter as she would help with a lot of the work. She had learned to type at college in Pau and she had bought a very rickety typewriter. When her mother died, she took over a lot. She would come in every morning and get her father dressed and do his breakfast and prepare lunch for him and Francis.

She wondered what was going on as Francis wasn't in the yard feeding the goats and chickens, and milking the house cow. She was worried as these things had to be done, and she was angry with Eloise as she just

THE SPIRITS OF PULHAMS MILL

disappeared for days on end, leaving Sarah to pick up the pieces. And now Francis wasn't about either. 'This isn't good enough,' she muttered to herself. 'I will end up having to do the farm work as well.'

The door of the kitchen flew open!!

Jean-Baptiste and Patrick, covered in blood, came through, carrying Eloise's body on a makeshift stretcher. They pushed the chairs away as Sarah cleared the table. She could see that Eloise had lost a lot of blood and was pale as death and realised that her sister had gone: her anger turned to an outburst of tears.

Her father, woken by the noise, could not believe his eyes; Eloise, his beautiful daughter, the image of his beloved wife, lying on the kitchen table dead. He rushed to try to bring her back.

He knew that it was futile! Jean-Baptiste held him as the tears brimmed in his eyes, and he fell in torment, the sobs coming from deep within him, shaking his whole body. This broke his heart. Jean-Baptiste had to hold him and stop him from collapsing.

'Where is my grandson?'

Sarah and Jean-Baptiste managed to move Pestone back to his chair by the fire. Sarah was still holding onto her father; both of them in shock, disbelief and grief, a pulsating presence in the room!

Patrick was able to think of the practical problems. He went to phone the gendarme, but the village switchboard, run by Madame Silvia, didn't answer, so he said that he would run over to the gendarmerie in the next village, and they would call Pau. Jean-Baptiste recovered himself and stopped him from going. They walked outside.

They had to get the story set so that everyone was singing from the same hymn sheet. They couldn't get away from the fact that Eloise had been shot. They couldn't tell the truth about how it had actually happened, but their story needed to be believable. There was bound to be a close investigation. They knew that if Francis was interrogated, he would break down and blurt out everything; it was best if he was nowhere to be found until everything calmed down. They had to decide if it would be best to cause a diversion! The project to blow up the railway line was planned, and if Eloise was shot as one of the perpetrators, that would be a very good cover story; as the Gestapo could not interrogate her, they would feel they had an important member of the Resistance and be satisfied that she was a martyr for their cause. The drawback to that was that they might take the whole family.

So, Sarah had to know and feed the information in such a way that they felt that she was a collaborator. He would have to use her husband as a conduit for this to work. There were a lot of villagers who hated the Vichy government. But who to trust? Patrick was not keen on this as he felt it was too complicated!

By the evening, Sarah had recovered enough for Jean-Baptiste and Patrick to be able to talk and reason with her. She was getting ready to go to her husband, who would be wondering what had happened to her and expecting her to make him supper. If she didn't go soon, he would be coming round to fetch her.

She wasn't stupid. She had picked up that Francis had something to do with this, but the scenario had to leave out Jerry and the cave! They invented the drama of Francis and Eloise looking for a mountain bear (they were still around, and they did occasionally take a sheep or a goat). Francis had taken a shot at a bear, and the bullet had ricocheted off a rock!

Sarah accepted this explanation at face value but asked, 'Where is my nephew, Francis? He must be in a terrible state. Why didn't you bring him back home?'

Jean-Baptiste explained. 'He couldn't deal with the grief. We stopped him from killing himself twice! He ran off like a fatally injured dog. The adrenaline took him. We couldn't catch him. The mountain rescue team are searching for him at the moment. We will go and join them and bring him home. We left it to the experts.'

After Sarah had left, Jean-Baptiste realised that Monsieur Pestone was still in shock, but he was fretting about Francis. They didn't tell him that Francis had shot his mother. They didn't want to add to his grief in his present state.

Sarah had prepared some food, and they took it through to the 'best room' to eat, away from the sight of devastation. After that, they helped Monsieur to bed. They covered Eloise and let the fire go out.

Patrick left to meet up with the rest of the group. They had decided that they would still cause this diversion and would go ahead with the plan that Eloise had so carefully planned.

Jean-Baptiste stayed to feed the animals and organised a neighbour, Monsieur François Soubirous, and the assistant *maire*, to help. He was a Resistance sympathiser, so Jean-Baptiste felt he could be trusted with some of the truth, but his wife, Bethrel, was a bit of a gossip, so he had to be very careful that the version of events was clear of any reference to Eloise being part of the Resistance. As the locals considered her a 'bit of girl,' Jean-Baptiste used this to explain how she was accidentally shot by a stray bullet. He managed to build the story of jealousy between lovers and that Francis had witnessed it and was understandably very traumatised by the death of his mother. François, now the acting *maire*, had to report the death to the gendarmerie.

(XIII)
THE BARN NEAR SAINT-GIRONS

So, Jean-Baptiste decided it was best if he disappeared. (He was not a local, so there might be some awkward questions) He would take some food and wine and find Francis and Jerry. It was a long walk, so he borrowed a motorbike from the neighbours.

He was travelling too fast on a very rocky track, came off and rolled down a grassy bank. He hit his head and lost consciousness for a short time, although he wasn't badly hurt, just a bit shaken; the bike was still running on the edge of the track, so he clambered up and put it back on its wheels. He just had to get to the barn as quickly as possible. He put his clumsiness down to the drama he had had to deal with. Bruised and battered (he had washed Eloise's blood off), he arrived at the barn before the sun went down. He had no idea how long all this had taken. He thought to himself, 'It's just as well it's summer.'

Francis was still very groggy from the amount of brandy they had forced down him. There was a camping stove and Jerry was making coffee. The appearance of a third person prompted Francis to wake from his torpor again. Looking with daggers at Jerry, he tried to get up and swing a punch at him. However, the movement was too much for him. He toppled over in a heap onto a straw bail and just lay there holding his head.

At that moment, Jerry realised that he could never make things right with Francis. This was war in occupied France, and he and Francis had been forced together by the circumstances. It was never going to be an easy relationship. It was a matter of life and death. If either of them stepped out of line, it would endanger the lives of many men and women in the Resistance. Jerry decided that Francis would try to kill him. So, Jean-Baptiste had to convince Frances that Jerry was very streetwise and was the only person they could rely on to enable their survival and escape to the UK.

Francis was now in a state of denial and disbelief. It was as if he was in a bad dream and his mother would walk in. Then the realisation that it was all true fell back on him like a ton of mud. He collapsed again, and Jerry went to hold him. Jean-Baptiste took control. He sat Francis down on a straw bale and sat beside him, holding him, allowing the tears to flow. He spoke in French, soothing and singing a local ballad that spoke of sorrow, regret, and redemption:

> *Je ne saurais imaginer ton supplice.*
> I can't imagine your torment.
> *Je sais qu'il y a de la lumière devant nous*
> I know there is light ahead
> *Si seulement tu pouvais la voir.*
> If you could but see it.
> *Ton regret et ta douleur sont presents*
> Your regret and sorrow is here
> *Et t'accompagneront toujours.*
> And will always be with you.
> *Tu ne peux pas t'en cacher.*
> You cannot hide from it.
> *Elle sait que tu l'aimes.*
> She knows that you love her.
> *Si elle le pouvait, elle tiendrait.*
> If she could, she would hold you.
> *Elle sécherait tes larmes et te dirait*
> She would dry your tears and tell you
> *Sa vie continue dans ton âme.*
> Her life lives on in your soul.

This seemed to help, and his tears became sobs. As he recovered, he was muttering that he had to get back to feed the animals and look after his grandfather. Jean-Baptiste had to tell Francis that he could not go back to the farm. This angered him.

'Why not? It's my home!'

'If you told the truth, this would be playing into the hands of the Vichy and the Germans.' He had to tell

Francis that Eloise was the head of a group, and she and Jerry were working for the Resistance. As Jerry had come to France to work against the Germans, Monsieur François Soubirous must not know that he had tried to kill Jerry and accidentally shot his mother as this would jeopardise many lives. He added, 'Monsieur Soubirous is on our side, but if he doesn't know the truth, then he can't let it slip when the gendarmes are investigating his mother's death.'

Through all his intense sorrow, Francis realised that this is what his mother would have wanted. 'But I will kill Jerry; the BASTARD must die'.'

Jean-Baptiste held Francis in a vice-like bear hug to stop him from taking his sorrow and hate out on Jerry.

'Francis, I know you want to kill Jerry, but he is your only chance of getting out of here alive and back to the UK. I know he is the cause of your mother's death. Eloise would want you to survive. Importantly, she would want you to work with him to defeat the Germans. Who are the *real* bastards? I don't expect you to be friends, but for the sake of the cause, bear with him. He has his own guilt and sorrow to handle. Like your mother, you are somehow bound to Jerry in a recurring bad dream. This is all I can say or do. If you are determined to kill him, that is up to you. Although he wants to help both of you to recover from this disaster. He will defend himself. He has killed before and won't hesitate to kill you if he has to. I implore you to see the consequences. I must leave you now to get our transport.'

Jean-Baptiste left and rode the motorbike to Saint-Girons and found his friend Christian. He had a Citroën van that he could borrow. He loaded the bike, and he went to pick up Jerry and Francis.

As he approached the barn, he heard what he thought was a German motorbike (they have a distinctive sound). He stopped behind a tree just below the horizon and walked to the top of the hill. There *was* a German bike parked outside. He very carefully approached and looked through the gaps in the woodwork. He could see a uniform, but it wasn't German. He recognised him as a Vichy sympathiser in a uniform he hadn't seen before. He was questioning Jerry, who had his hand in his pocket. From this angle, he could see that he was about to shoot him. Francis was nowhere to be seen.

Jean-Baptiste took control and called out in French, 'What are you doing in my barn?' to attract the intruders' attention.

This broke the tension, and the monsieur turned, and as he did so, Jerry shot him. He didn't die immediately. This was not good news as it is difficult to finish a job half done.

Surprisingly, Francis appeared from behind a straw bale and produced a knife and cut the intruder's throat! This was a complete shock to the others. It seemed to be a reaction to all the drama that had poured itself on him in the previous 24 hours.

They had to wait until daylight to dispose of the body and the motorbike. Jean-Baptiste had walked this part of the Pyrenees and had been shown a brown bear's den not far from the barn. They managed to park the bike at the back of the bear's den. Between them, they carried the body to a place in the den where the bear had killed a deer, and left it there in the hope that the bear would find it and destroy any evidence. They didn't really think about it, but had the bear returned while they were doing this, they would have been in real trouble. It was time to leave, Jerry on the motorbike, to join the group at Sarrance.

Jean-Baptiste was pretty certain that Francis was in a fit state to return to the farm. Although he was very withdrawn, he assured Jean that he understood the delicacy of the situation; he knew that the whole family could be arrested and handed over to the Gestapo. This, on its own, was enough to keep him from losing it. He loved his grandfather and needed the support of Sarah, his aunt.

They drove slowly in the Citroën over very rough ground and arrived to find Sarah cooking a chicken. It was Sunday. The previous day the gendarmes had been and taken Eloise's body away. They were going to question Francis on the Monday morning.

Jean-Baptiste was now the leader of his group, so he needed to make sure that the plan that he and Eloise had hatched worked. So, he had a very quick bite to eat and left to pick up some weapons and explosives from a secret dump by a very circuitous route.

(XIV)
THE RAILWAY LINE AT SARRANCE

The group comprising Henry, Gabriel and Daniel made their way separately to Monsieur Lefèvre's farm at Latapie (his son had been taken by the Vichy gendarmes). The farm was close to the railway line through the Somport Tunnel and a very important bridge, le Pont de l'Estanquet.

They had changed Eloise's plan. She had decided that it was better to blow up a connecting bridge that would be very difficult to repair rather than to close the tunnel which was being used as an escape route by rail to Pamplona (which was very anti-Nazi). There was a two-way trade of information, and the headquarters of the beleaguered PSOE was there.

Jean-Baptiste arrived at the farm around midday. His watch had been broken during the drama of the last few days. Henry and Daniel helped unload the explosives and detonators to check them through and prepare them.

Mme Lefèvre had prepared lunch. The group were very upset about the loss of Eloise, but they accepted Jean-Baptiste as the natural successor. Gabriel was not saying a word, but it was obvious that he was not happy. He started an argument stating, 'It should never have been run by a woman.' He felt that he should be the top dog.

A dog barked!

They stepped away from the table and against the wall. Drawing their weapons, Mme Lefèvre called her husband to see if anyone had arrived. Jerry, being Jerry, came through the back scullery accompanied by Monsieur Lefèvre. Gabriel would nearly have shot him had it not been for Daniel, who was standing next to him and recognised Jerry, to knock the gun out of his hand. It was lucky that the pistol didn't go off anyway. They were understandably very nervous!

Gabriel said, 'What's he doing here. I thought he was going on the escape route back to where he came from!' But the others ignored this outburst.

Things settled down, and Jerry sat down at the table with them as they ate and drank Monsieur Lefèvre's cider. This had a calming effect on them, partially on Gabriel, who was a drinker. They were able to get down to planning how to blow up the bridge. Gabriel was an important factor in this plan as he had been in the army and had handled explosives on several other occasions with this group.

It was a fine day, but they took the explosives into the shed to set them up. Although the farm was isolated, they couldn't risk a passing neighbour seeing what they were doing. Jerry, being the youngest and the fittest, volunteered to do the most dangerous job. He had to be instructed on how to do it. If the explosion didn't go evenly and in sequence, it could jeopardise the whole plan. He was a quick learner but sometimes thought he knew best.

When it was set up, they packed it back in the Citroën van, and it all piled in as well. Jean-Baptiste drove carefully to the middle of a very thick, overgrown hedge very close to the bridge. Normally they would have waited till dark, but it was summer and didn't get dark until 9 p.m. And in any case, the train was due at 4.50 p.m., so they had to take the chance that they wouldn't be seen by the locals. They surveyed the area very carefully.

It was all quiet after lunch as the farmers retired for an hour, sometimes more, in the hot summer. The Nazis had not guarded this bridge yet; they still considered the Resistance to be an irritation rather than a threat. Jerry took the box of Nobel 808 explosives in eight brown paper boxes, and four specially made limpet mines and tape in his backpack and walked innocently across the path and sat down as if he was considering fishing. He slid down to the water's edge near the steel support and tied one box on each side of the support, pushing a detonator wire into each. He repeated this on the next support. He couldn't believe his luck; there was a small punt tied up by the riverbank, which he boarded, taking the wire with him, stretching it tight and above the water and out of sight below the centre of the track.

He punted across to the other supports and repeated the process. Then he pulled himself up under and attached the limpet mines to both main frames of the bridge. Then it was hand over hand back to where he had started. He put the roll of wire in his pack and walked back to the hedge to the others.

The time was getting on, but they still had to wait for the train. This was where it could all go wrong. They had to stay alert and be ready for the unexpected. They sat with their automatic weapons at the ready and brewed coffee to keep themselves awake. The time dragged on, on that hot July afternoon. While they were waiting, Monsieur Lefèvre appeared with a wheelbarrow full of gravel and spread it over the wire as it crossed the path.

Time stood still while they waited for the train to get to the bridge.

At last …

They let the engine and the first four carriages cross the bridge, and as the last open truck and the guards van with the troops guarding the military equipment came onto the bridge, they detonated! The bridge collapsed, taking with it the rear rolling stock and breaking the couplings to the front and the engine, which luckily stayed on the track but slid back to the edge. The wreckage of the bridge stopped them from toppling over.

The brakes came on automatically. What was left of the train ground to a screeching halt!

Jean-Baptiste and Daniel had set up a machine gun. They held their fire. This confused the German guards as they recovered from the shock of what had just happened; they jumped down dazed but wary, not knowing from which side of the remaining carriages they were likely to be attacked.

Jerry Henry and Gabriel had set up on the other side. They didn't want any of the guards to escape.

There was a big silence! Everyone was holding their breath!

At last, a German corporal thought he saw a movement and took a shot; this provoked a hail of bullets from the guards. As there was no return fire, they felt that there was no threat, so they started to move about. This, of course, was fatal!

Daniel opened fire, and eight guards dived for cover under the train. Three succeeded, but they were cut down as they rolled under and out on the other side of the rolling stock. The driver and his mate came down with their hands up! The carriage that had hit the wreckage of the bridge was derailed, so it was not possible to move the train!

There didn't seem to be any further movement, but there were maybe 25 passengers in those carriages, so Jerry and Gabriel climbed aboard and checked out if they were armed. Henry and Daniel surveyed the carnage they had caused. There were sounds coming from the guard's van, and two soldiers, in a sorry state, dragged themselves to the top of the riverbank and collapsed.

The rail authorities would arrive soon, so the saboteurs decided that it was time to go! The explosion would have attracted attention for miles around. They collected their kit and drove over the fields. They didn't go back to the farm as they didn't want Monsieur Lefèvre to be implicated.

Soon the Gestapo would be there. The high command was not going to be best pleased. The harm done by this derailment was not obvious at first sight. The supply of tungsten from Spain was a vital ingredient for the German army. This line through the Pyrenees was kept a very low profile to avoid aerial bombardment.

The group split up and decided to meet up again in three days' time, about 30 km away in the village of

Arudy, at Monsieur Perinée's, above the café. This was useful as it could be accessed from the rear through a field and a passageway.

Jerry and Jean-Baptiste drove the Citroën van to a secret location, La Grange, near the Château d'Izeste to unload the explosives and machine gun. They made their way back on foot to check to see if Francis and his father were still at liberty.

(XV)
PESTONE'S FARM AT BUZIET NEAR ARUDY, TWO DAYS LATER

They arrived to find the local priest, Father Joseph, and all the neighbours lining up behind two horse-drawn hearses moving off towards the church. This was a double funeral for Monsieur Pestone and his daughter, Eloise. Both Jerry and Jean-Baptiste joined the procession at a little distance, keeping a very low profile. Francis, Sarah, and Monsieur Soubirous were just behind the hearse with Father Joseph. As they approached the church, there was a German half-track troop carrier in the square and about ten German soldiers watching. The *Oberleutnant* halted the procession, demanding to search the hearses.

Father Joseph and Monsieur Soubirous both barred his way.

They were not going to allow these interlopers to desecrate this holy occasion. The officer was taken aback by this. He didn't know what to do next. He couldn't lose face in front of his men. He started to move them out of his way, pushing them with his weapon, and the tension grew as there was a standoff.

The local gendarme came to the rescue. He spoke enough German to explain that it would not be good for his relationship with the cooperative authorities. He would guarantee that there was no reason the town *maire*'s funeral would be a problem. The tension relaxed, and the procession proceeded into the church. It happened that the officer was a Catholic, so he respected the priest.

Jean-Baptiste and Jerry followed and sat down in a pew at the front of a side chapel. Francis acknowledged them. Virtually all the pews were taken. The locals were all paying their respects, and the service was very long as a mass was celebrated. Father Joseph gave a very politically correct sermon. He included a lot of pointed remarks that had more than one meaning in French that would go over the heads of the Germans. There was a lot of unhappiness about the Vichy government and their capitulation to the Nazis, but there were also many sympathisers in the town.

Jerry and Jean-Baptiste left by a side door before the end of the service. They could see the German soldiers having a smoke. Before they were seen, they withdrew and decided to wait till the service was finished, and left in the confusion along with the rest of the congregation. They slipped away into a back street. When all was quiet again, they made their way back to the farm, keeping away from roads. They stayed overnight in a barn and arrived just as it was getting dark so they were sure they wouldn't meet up with locals paying their respects to the *maire* and his daughter.

To their surprise, Sarah welcomed them just as Francis arrived in from feeding and bedding down the animals. She laid out some dishes and some bread for chabròl and cheese.

The atmosphere was not exactly happy, but under the circumstances, it was relatively civil and friendly. The conversion was not about their losses. It seemed that Sarah had become privy to the fact that Eloise was a leader of a group in the Resistance. They talked in the Euskara dialect about the bridge being blown up. Jerry had gathered a lot of French but had no idea what they were saying now, and Jean-Baptiste was trying to translate it, but it was very near to Spanish, so he found it difficult. It was very useful. Most of the Basque people hated the northern French, let alone Germans, and they certainly hated the Vichy and all they stood for.

Sarah was telling them that her husband, Pierre, had been arrested as a Resistance suspect. He was very angry and now wanted to join a group. It was difficult to recruit him as a lot of locals thought he was in favour of Pétain because of some of his associates. He knew that Eloise was part of a group, and he wasn't going to put his family in danger. He also knew that Jerry was British. After they had eaten, they packed some bread and wine, and Jerry and Jean-Baptiste left and made their way to the barn, Les Granges du Bénou, a secret place to sleep. They had to keep Jerry away just in case the authorities discovered his real identity. His French wasn't good enough yet. Neither Sarah nor Francis knew about this barn. This was to keep them safe. If they didn't know its whereabouts, there was less chance of them accidentally mentioning it if they were questioned.

(XVI)
ABOVE MONSIEUR ALBERT PERINÉE'S CAFÉ

The next day they walked to Arudy for the meeting. They arrived in time for some lunch. Henry, Gabriel and Daniel were all seated. Food always came first, but that was just as well as in three days, they had only had cheese, bread and wine. Albert seated them and served them the dish of the day, Garbure et Poule au Pot, which they ate in total silence. This might be their last meal. They were always on the edge of disaster, but it didn't stop them from enjoying a good meal. They were quietly celebrating the destruction of the bridge, and they had all survived to meet today.

Gabriel said, 'We have to be very careful when we leave. There is a Vichy gendarme that Albert thinks is watching the café. When he is off duty, he just sits drinking black coffee, and he hardly talks to anyone. Albert has asked him if he has trouble at home, but unlike most of his customers, he just grunts and has more coffee. The locals don't know him very well as he has only recently been posted here from Toulouse.'

With the loss of Eloise as their leader, they had not made any plans for future assignments, but they all voted for Jean-Baptiste as her replacement.

Henry asked, 'How is Francis? This is a terrible thing to live with! I cannot imagine the guilt. To live with the horror of such a thing. If I had done this, I would have killed myself!'

'We must pray for him to forgive himself.'

Jean-Baptiste said, 'Is there anything we can do? I hear that his grandfather died of a broken heart, so Francis is alone on the farm. As I only live 10 km away from him, when the heat of our last action has died down, I will go and help him on the farm.'

'If he will let me, I will stay with him until you have planned the next move,' offered Jerry.

But Gabriel said, 'This man is a danger to our group. He needs to go back to England! If he is arrested, they will immediately know he is not French.'

Jean-Baptiste, defending Jerry, said, 'As long as he is with us, he is an asset, and the fact that he is not French is an advantage. The Nazis cannot use his family to frighten him into giving away our groups.'

Jerry said, 'I have nothing to lose! I am a deserter from the British army. If I go back, I may well be shot! So, I can use my criminal knowledge to your advantage. I owe it to Eloise and Francis to do all I can to help you in the war against the Nazis.'

Jean-Baptiste said, 'Jerry was very useful on the bridge. Are we all agreed that we should lie low for a month? I will do a bit of research as to the best action we can take to upset both the Vichy and the Nazis. We will meet again in the barn at du Bénou.'

Then Henry and Daniel left the table. Daniel made his way into the café as if he had been to the toilet and sat at the same table as the gendarme, who ignored him at first. This was a good move; he engaged him in conversation, which took his attention away from the others leaving.

Daniel bought him a drink and asked him where he was from!

'I'm away from my family! My wife is pregnant and about to give birth, but they won't give me leave!' He was very disenchanted with the Vichy.

Daniel sympathised with him and asked Albert to bring some absinthe. Daniel just sat and drank, and after about 20 minutes, he left, telling the gendarme, 'I have to take my dog to the vet'. Daniel walked the 5 km to his home in the next village.

There were a lot of German cars around. A troop carrier was parked in front of the church of Église Saint-Germain. A staff car arrived, and the senior Gestapo officers marched into the town hall and took over the *maire*'s office. They set up an HQ for the investigation into the explosion and destruction of the railway bridge. Six non-commissioned officers and two Oberleutnant Gestapo arrived in separate transports. This was going to be an intensive search to find the saboteurs.

Jean-Baptiste and Jerry walked away, relaxed and chatting. One of the soldiers stopped them, and they produced their papers (Jerry's papers were a very good forgery). The soldier scrutinised them, compared the men to their photos, grunted and waved them on. They walked to the farm at Buziet, using unmade tracks to avoid the roads as much as possible.

Francis was there when they arrived. He said that Jerry could sleep in the barn if he helped on the farm. That was fine by Jerry as he didn't want to endanger the family. Francis had been interrogated by the local gendarme. They had accepted the explanation backed up by Sarah, that it was a terrible accident. The animals had to be fed, and the hay was brought in from the fields, so Francis got on with the life he had known for 20 years. He did have periods of anger and depression, but he understood that life had to go on without his mother. Jean-Baptiste stayed for a week to help and then went back to his family.

(XVII)
TABAC /CAFÉ, PLACE DE LA MAIRIE, BUZIET

Jerry was becoming accepted as a sort of tramp who spoke French with a very strange accent. He started going to the café and drinking absinthe. To begin with he would pretend to go to sleep in a drunken stupor if the gendarme arrived. Unusually for Jerry, he was dropping his guard. He felt at home there; for the first time in his life, he had friends whom he trusted.

Daniel joined him one Friday afternoon and as they discussed the next move, in English, they suddenly realised that there was someone eavesdropping, and they were very shocked.

Then Jean Soulages joined them at their table and said very quietly in French, 'You should be careful. It's a good job that I am not a Pétainiste, or you would have been in big trouble. I'll buy a bottle of wine, and we could go to my place.'

Jerry's luck was still holding! As they crossed the Place de la Mairie and had just turned into a lane, a German truck roared up, and 20 SS troops took up positions around the square as a Mercedes staff car swept to a halt. An SS officer led a group of men into the *tabac*. The troops dragged poor Monsieur Colinette, the barman, out protesting and marched him over to the *mairie*. They pounded on the door until the gendarme, looking very frightened, opened the door. They virtually knocked him over as they pushed past him.

Jerry, Daniel and Jean didn't wait to find out what was going on. They hurried to Jean's house. From the balcony, they had a view of the square. Jerry remembered what had happened to his only friend. He wanted to go over there and 'kill the bastards!' but discretion being the better part of valour, he calmed down and thought to himself that 'revenge is a pie best consumed cold.' His anger was re-emerging and directed at the Nazis.

There was little they could do to help Monsieur Colinette. They just hoped that they would realise that he had very little information and would then probably frighten him into becoming an informer. This could be useful as the group could feed false information. Jerry and Daniel were due to meet up with the group to plan their next endeavour.

(XVIII)
THE BARN DU BÉNOU

Jean-Baptiste was there when Daniel and Jerry arrived. They settled down to cleaning their automatics. They had them all in pieces when the oak door opened, and Gabriel arrived with two gendarmes with pistols drawn.

Daniel asked, *'Mais bon sang, qu'est-ce qui se passe, Gabriel?'*

Jerry seemed to have disappeared but came up behind them and shot Gabriel, who fell against one of the gendarmes, knocking him to the ground. In the confusion, Jean-Baptiste was able to pick up a lump of stone and hurl it at the other gendarme, hitting him on the head and knocking him to the ground. But Gabriel wasn't dead! He rolled off the gendarme and picked up his pistol. Before he collapsed, he took a shot at Jerry. This hit him in the chest, but as he hit the ground, his pistol went off, and the bullet passed through Gabriel's hand, so he dropped the pistol. Daniel had picked up an automatic he had just put together and loaded it as the door burst open. He shot Gabriel again and the gendarme, in one burst.

Jean-Baptiste cried, *'Quel gâchis! Pourquoi tu n'es pas mort, Gabriel?* What a mess! Why are you not dead, Gabriel? *Toi, bâtard!'* You bastard!

THE AUCTION ROOM

Jean-Baptiste ripped Jerry's shirt open. They could see that he was badly injured and bleeding profusely. The bullet had passed just above his heart. They managed to stem the bleeding and moved him to an old mattress in the corner and sat him up!

Daniel was about to put another shot into Gabriel, but he wanted to know if the Germans were on their way. He wasn't long for this world. Both Jean-Baptiste and Daniel could not believe that their school friend would have betrayed them. They were going to leave him there, but they decided it would be better to move him and dump him with the other dead gendarmes in a different location as this barn was very secluded. Gabriel was the only one who would have known how to find it. It was unlikely that Gabriel would survive the move as he was very close to death.

Jerry was in a bad way, but Daniel had been a medic in the army and had managed to dress the wound. They had a Citroën van and a 2CV hidden in the woods. The best way to go in separate directions. They loaded the bodies and the fading Gabriel into the van, and Daniel drove about 15 km to Uzein, near an airfield being used by the Germans. This was to move suspicion away from Buziet. On the way, Gabriel died. Daniel wanted to know why Gabriel had betrayed them. Gabriel had scrawled a note explaining why in blood on a scrap of paper, but it wasn't legible at first glance.

There was a perfect burial place, tangled woodland, and a hidden deep ditch at the end of the overgrown runway. The only person likely to go near there would be the grass cutter (who would probably hate the Pétain gendarmes anyway). The prevailing wind meant that aircraft very rarely took off in this direction. As they dumped the bodies, the note fell out. Daniel put it in his pocket. It was time to leave as he could hear an army truck bouncing across a field about a kilometre away.

(XIX)
PESTONE'S FARM AT BUZIET NEAR ARUDY

Jean-Baptiste managed to get Jerry into the 2CV. He drove very gently to Pestone's farm. Francis was in the yard when they arrived.

'Not him back again!'

But they were bonded together by their shared love of Eloise. So, although Francis still blamed Jerry, they were still in mourning. But Francis had a little guilty enjoyment causing Jerry some pain as he tried to remove the bullet which had hit his collarbone and broken it. Francis had begun to study to be a vet, so he had some medical knowledge. He couldn't dig too deep as Jerry had lost a lot of blood. Between them, they managed to carry him upstairs but were worried that a sympathiser might call around.

Francis wanted to join the Resistance and follow in his mother's footsteps. He had found a neighbour's son and his sister, Charlotte, to help on the farm, but it was difficult to know if they were Pétainistes or not, so he had to be careful when they were around. Jean-Baptiste teased him as he could see that Francis was very attracted to Charlotte, but as is often the case, her father didn't approve. It felt like history repeating itself. However, Francis felt that he could not commit to loving a woman who was nearly as beautiful as Eloise had been.

He wanted to return from England and train in Charles de Gaulle's Free France Army. He was making plans to leave the farm with his sister, Sarah.

There was, of course, his cousin, who had always wanted to come from Cahors on the River Lot and live in the Pyrenees. So, he wrote a letter to Bernard. He did think of sending a telegram, but he would have had to go to Buziet to send it, and he was too busy preparing to go. Like his mother, once he had made the decision to go, that was it! It would just take a few days to put everything together. Bernard had always been so keen to come here that Francis was convinced that he would just come straight away. His wife had recently left him as she blamed him for the car accident in which their two sons had died (the demon drink!).

Sarah was not very happy that Francis wasn't going to leave her the farm. But Francis didn't want Pierre, her husband, to take it over. So, five days later, when Bernard arrived unannounced, the problem was solved. Jerry was improving and didn't want to stay on at the farm, so Jean-Baptiste made the arrangements for him and Francis to leave through Marseille. They had been able to contact the SOE by radio.

(XX)
TRIP TO MARSEILLE

There was a submarine, the HMS *Dolphin*, in the Med. due to pick up an important French intelligence colonel of the Free France Army who had been stranded. If Francis could get them to the hidden bay at Les Calanques, just outside Marseille in ten days, they would be lifted from the beach out to the submarine, which would surface under the cliffs. It could only be there for 20 minutes maximum.

Francis, accompanied by Jean-Baptiste, was in his De-cheviot, and Jerry and Daniel were in the Citroën van, along with Patrick, who had caught up with them on his Rhony'X motorbike (not suitable for off-road). They made their way using back roads and tracks that were only known by locals.

They took eight days to do the trip, stopping at night in out-of-the-way barns that their Resistance contacts had told them about. They were doing very well. Occasionally Patrick would go into a village and find food and some of the local wine. Mostly the farmers along the way would offer them a barn to sleep in. On the last occasion, the farmer's wife, Mme Bridgete, insisted all four of them stay for a slap-up meal and a bed for the night. They were only a day away from Les Calanques and were a day early. It was just as well as they had too much wine that night!

Jerry was in a lot of pain as the bullet was still lodged near his collarbone, and the road trip had moved it about. In the morning, while they were all in bed, Mme

THE AUCTION ROOM

Bridgete cycled to the village and brought the local doctor to look at his wound. The doctor concluded that it was best to leave the bullet where it was. He injected penicillin and some painkillers into the wound and gave Mme Bridgete his bill and left. Jerry had a bad feeling about the doctor, so he paid Madame immediately.

He told the others about his bad feelings and persuaded them to pack up and leave. His premonition proved on the nail. They had only gone 10 km when, down in the valley, they saw a convoy of German trucks. There was no way that they could combat that many. They stopped and hid the vehicles off the road in woodland and set up a trap just in case they had to fight. The trucks headed directly to Mme Bridgete's farm, but they took a shortcut and missed them altogether. Jerry's luck was still holding!

Patrick had been given a route along an old disused Roman road that would bypass Marseille. They had to get to close to the rendezvous before dark and were worried that they might have let on where they were headed. Patrick went on ahead on his motorbike to reconnoitre the scene and find a place where they could hide the vehicles and sleep the night. He found a cave where they had a view of the bay. It was a point where they could see the signal light from the submarine that was going to arrive at 11 p.m. the next night. They slept in a tangled wood where they had hidden the vehicles 500 metres away from the coast.

Jerry and Francis took a walk to the top of the cliffs. As they rounded an outcrop, this stunning view of the coast was revealed: the azure calm sea, with a couple of fishing boats returning to port. It was hard to believe there was a war going on all around them. This scene of tranquillity had such a calming effect on Francis that he began to cry and let out all the grief of the last few months. Jerry's tears joined his, and they held each other until the tears subsided as the sun went down.

The next day dragged on as they waited till the evening. Patrick went into Morgiou village to buy some bread, cheese, and local cider. There didn't seem to be any wine. He gave the café people the impression that he had a boat anchored in the harbour but did not say too much. They would be gone tomorrow.

There was a new moon and at about 10.30 p.m., Jean-Baptiste was on watch for the signal. Patrick and Daniel arranged a trap along the path so that if any unwanted troops appeared, they could hold them off. All was quiet by 10.45 p.m. Francis and Jerry were on the beach when out of the dark came an armed escort and a grey-haired official-looking man (the intelligence colonel). The escort challenged Jerry, but when he spoke English, they were happy. There was a signal from Jean-Baptiste. They waited about ten minutes, and out of the darkness, there emerged a rubber dinghy with three sailors in black waterproofs that beached silently. They handed each of them dark waterproofs. Jerry said he wasn't going, but the sailor with pistols insisted that they had to pick up three passengers, so he had no choice. Just as they boarded the submarine, there was gunfire.

Francis and Jerry could do nothing about that.

The first officer welcomed them aboard and evacuated the conning tower with the crew sliding down the ladders and closing all the hatches. The coxswain showed them to their cramped bunks. A warning klaxon sounded as the floor sloped away forward, and the sub dived.

The French colonel tripped and fell into the captain's cabin.

Jerry had about ten days to sort out his future. He was bound to be arrested when they realised who he was. For the moment, he had his French identity, which had been held under the scrutiny of both the Germans and the gendarmes:

Monsieur Gerald Fabrigard
23 Av. Gaston Phoebus, Pau, France

Francis managed to talk to the French colonel about joining General de Gaulle's Free France Army, but he didn't get much encouragement (apparently, this rather arrogant man thought it was beneath him to deal with it).

The German Navy had not really taken control of the south of France or the Med Ports in 1941. The HMS *Dolphin* surfaced and entered Gibraltar to take on supplies. They would surface again off Plymouth and offload their passengers before their patrol in the Atlantic for about 25 days.

CHAPTER 9

Jerry's Winzor's Story – Part 3

THE RETURN
DEVONPORT DOCKS 54, A SMALL
UNOBTRUSIVE LANDING STAGE

The pinnace came alongside the HMS *Dolphin* off Stonehouse. As soon as the passengers were safely unloaded and the tender had cleared the area, the submarine headed out and disappeared into a rainstorm, which rocked the pinnace as it headed for land with a following wind. Francis had been feeling seasick as the sub waited for the tender; it was rocking in the long swell. As he boarded the tender, feeling dizzy, he slipped and fell heavily but was saved from injury by a crewman. Jerry managed to get him to the other side, so he was sick to leeward. By the time they arrived, Francis had recovered. The French colonel was not very pleased as he had received some vomit on his face.

Jerry and Francis had to wait until the colonel had been received by some top French brass – Jerry thought he recognised General de Gaulle in civilian clothes. The whole entourage then disappeared out of the rain very quickly.

To begin with, Jerry and Francis were treated like prisoners until a suited man took control and escorted them to a black car. Jerry could not believe it as they headed towards Exeter and onto Bampton.

(II)
VENNE HOUSE NEAR BROMPTON REGIS, SOMERSET

They arrived at an obscure but large country house, which was about half a mile from where Francis was born at Ditch Farm. They were escorted through a door in an overgrown garden wall to reveal the hidden Palladian mansion and then in through a side door and a passageway. They were shown into separate rooms to be debriefed.

Jerry could not let on that he was a local, or, for the moment, that he was English.

The door opened, and a craggy but strangely attractive woman entered. She offered him a seat and sat at the other side of the table.

'Who are you?'

'Vous avez mes papiers.' You have my papers.

Moira, for that was the woman's name, said again in English, 'You don't fool me. That's not a French accent.'

'I'm Canadian. I went to Paris to find my family and was caught up in the invasion.'

'Try again! I detect a Somerset accent!'

'OK. I've been in France fighting with the Resistance for months and saving British airmen's lives.'

'So, who are you?'

'That is a very esoteric question. Basically, I am a different person to the one who left England months ago!'

'You realise that when we find out, you will probably be hung as a spy or traitor. Or I could just take you out to the yard and shoot you myself now!'

'You won't because I could be very useful to you.'

Moira stood up and walked out, slamming the door, which locked after her. In the next room, Francis was explaining who he was. And that he wanted to join the Free France Army. This was accepted.

Moira was trying to find out more about Jerry (Gerald Fabrigard) next door. Francis didn't know his French name. He only knew him as Jerry, as that was short for

Gerald, and this confused Moira, so she was no further ahead. Jerry had chosen his French name well.

After an hour or so, they were both allowed to leave the cell-like rooms and escorted to the great hall, which was set up as a canteen. It was dinner time so there was a large hatchway /counter with steaming dishes of food. The hall had four tables that were occupied by a mixture of uniformed and civilian men and women. Francis and Jerry took a plate each and helped themselves to what looked like an Irish stew and overcooked boiled potatoes and veg – boarding school fare. They were hungry, so they sat down at a table with two civilian ladies who welcomed them with smiles.

Julia said in French, 'Welcome to a very English institution.' She apparently knew who they were. Then in English, 'We all know what is going on and who is who here. This is Gillian, and I am Julia. We are both in the decryption department. You've already met Moira. She thinks she's the boss. The actual boss, Benjamin Bolsover, or BB, isn't here at the moment. He doesn't often dine with us. Too important! Are you staying here, or are you being boarded out?'

Although Francis understood fluent English, he hadn't acclimatised yet.

Jerry said, 'I think here we have no choice in the matter. If all the girls are as good-looking as you two, though, our stay here is going to be enjoyable! It's good to talk to people who aren't interrogating us. I'm Jerry, and the good-looking one is Francis. He does speak English but is more comfortable in his native French.'

The girls did the French thing of shaking hands. They had to leave as their lunch break was over. They both got up at the same time, and the bench they were sitting on was upended. Jerry was tipped onto the floor, so several people came to his rescue, including Moira, who commented, 'That wasn't very smart of you,' as she helped him up. 'You will be staying in the house for a week while we sort out what you can do for us. We do realise that you are Jerry Winzor. When you have finished your meal, Mather here will show you both to your sleeping quarters.

'OK! There is a social area where you can meet others and listen to the radio at the front of the house – it's the door to the left of the front door. Don't get too comfortable, as you may not be here long.

'Francis, you will start training tomorrow. You will be woken at 7 a.m. Breakfast is from 7.30 to 8.30 a.m., and there will be a further debriefing first thing and then an introduction to your team. You may meet BB tomorrow.'

By now, they were both tired and were glad to get their heads down.

(III)
PULHAMS MILL, BROMPTON REGIS

Bertie and Joyce had moved out of the Mill to Broom Cottage when Betty died. Fred Hancock, who owned it, had left it to his daughter, Joyce. When Francis had finished being debriefed, John Hancock allowed him to move back to the Mill. There was some doubt as to John's ownership as the deeds had never been transferred from Eloise Pestone. As the bungalow was empty, John was happy to have Eloise's son move back in. He was not so keen that Jerry wanted to move in! This might not be a problem, though, as Jerry had been offered two alternatives by BB: go back to France or be arrested as a deserter.

Jerry was keen to go back to France and carry on where he had left off, but there was a problem! The bullet that had been lodged below his collarbone had migrated and was now very close to his spine and was giving him a lot of pain. The doctors didn't want to try and remove it as it was in a very dangerous position. The only surgeon able to do it was very busy with war-wounded. Jerry was not a priority. There was a good chance that he would end up in a wheelchair anyway.

(IV)
BACK AT VENNE HOUSE, UPTON, SOMERSET

Jerry's luck this time was a double-edged sword. Moira, whose husband (an air commodore) had been killed in an air crash two years before, had fallen for Jerry. She had the power to keep him out of prison. Although Jerry was attracted to this powerful woman, he didn't want to be tied down. It was obvious that his condition would stop him from being sent on active duty. It might be that if Moira could get Mr Pemberton, her father, to do the operation, then Jerry might be fit again. She was reluctant as she didn't want him to go back to France. It was difficult to be certain if this was a control thing or if she didn't want to lose another man she cared for: probably a mixture of both.

Francis was undergoing intensive training in hand-to-hand fighting with knives and aggressive judo, handling a pistol and target practice. He was a fit, strong farmer's son. Killing animals for food was one thing but knifing or shooting another human was altogether different. He had no problem with language as he was a native French speaker; he didn't need a special identity. The training officers decided that it would be good to organise one, anyway, so he could distance himself from his family if the Gestapo were to capture him. He was to be sent back in and make contact with Jean-Baptiste again. He was now a very important link with the Resistance.

As Jerry couldn't go back into active service, he was taken on by the SOE as a trainer in criminal techniques such as breaking and entering, deception, avoiding arrest and escape. These were the things that had kept him safe for the time he had been in France. The most important asset was being flexible and converting a bad situation into an opportunity.

He was allowed to leave Venne and live out. He tried to move back to Ditch Farm. In a very short time, it had almost fallen down, and the owner didn't care. He was going to try to replace the roof and rebuild the stone walls. The owner, Bill Buckingham, knew the old Jerry. Bill thought that Jerry was a coward who had avoided going to the trenches with all the young village men who had been lost. His son, Peter, was one of them.

He came one day as Jerry was doing some drystone walling. Bill was a miserable old codger who didn't want anyone on his property, even if it was being improved. He fired some buckshot over Jerry's head, shouting, 'Get off my land, or the next one will be in your chest!'

Jerry knew that when he couldn't win, he left.

He knew that Francis was only going to be at the Mill for about two weeks. He returned to Venne and had supper with Francis, who told him he was due to be parachuted into northern France in four days' time. This was a bit of a shock. Jerry had become like a replacement father to Francis. They were bound to each other by events. Jerry was very concerned that he was not properly prepared. The following day he was going for two days to Dunkeswell for parachute training. Francis was very nervous about this as he had never been in a plane, let alone jumped out of one at 4,000 feet. It was difficult for Jerry to reassure him as he had never flown either. As usual, he bluffed his way through!

Francis wanted Jerry to go to Dunkeswell with him, but Moira had other plans for Jerry. He had to tutor a course in developing escape and avoidance techniques. With his record of getting away with his life in very difficult situations, he was well-placed to do this. Francis was accompanied by a very experienced parachutist, so he was reassured.

On his return, he seemed very confident and ready to do the jump two days later. Jerry felt a responsibility for him, but he needn't have worried as although Francis was nervous, he was up for it as he boarded the transport to take him to an unnamed airfield in Kent. Jerry hugged him, and he was gone.

(V)
PULHAMS MILL, 1942

Jerry Winzor and Moira Pemberton had settled into a routine. As Venne House was only about a ten-minute cycle ride away, they had convinced John Hancock that Francis was happy for them to move in. It was quite possible that he would not return until after the war. This was a very open-ended situation as the war was not going well for Britain at the time. No one could admit that the outcome could be anything but positive. Moira was very busy as BB had been recalled to Whitehall to brief Churchill on the work they were doing in this very isolated secret establishment.

As the Mill was so close to Venne, she did get time to spend with Jerry. They were getting to be like a married couple. Moira's father did not approve of Jerry. He had found out about Jerry's history, but he was so busy in London working at St Thomas' just on the other side of the river to the Houses of Parliament. Even he didn't know where his daughter was working as it was top secret. The security people had an unfounded suspicion that he was a Nazi sympathiser. They threatened Moira with consequences if she gave her father any information, particularly about Venne. One other establishment had been bombed, and they suspected that a member of the staff had leaked information about it. Moira was happy for the moment with her bad boy partner.

This was the longest relationship Jerry had sustained in his life. He knew it wouldn't last forever. But true to form, he went along with it. Although very short-lived, his interlude with Eloise was still the most important, and being at the Mill kept it alive. He did miss the cut and thrust of his time with the Resistance, though. The bullet lodged near his collarbone was painful at times, but it didn't stop him from going back to his roots and farming the 30 acres that went with the Mill.

Life continued as it had for centuries.

The Spirits had been quiet as they approved and had no problem with the occupiers of the Mill who were in tune with them.

(VI)
A FIELD NEAR CHAMBORD, FRANCE, AUGUST 1942

Francis Pestone landed on the top of a small tree on the edge of a wooded valley. Luck was with him, as had he landed 2 metres north, he would have fallen into a very deep pond on the floor of the valley. Although it was dark, he managed to disconnect his harness and dropped to the ground about 3 metres below him. He knew that it was important to gather the parachute together and bury it so it didn't show up in the moonlight.

It was a very dark night, but as he was disposing of the parachute, he saw a very dim light approaching him. He had no time to hide. It was OK; it was his welcoming party. Without a word, they helped him and handed him a coat. Then they gave him a suitcase with all the necessary kit he would need to appear like a visitor about to catch a train. The four of them then piled into a 2CV and drove him across two fields and onto the main road to Poitiers to catch a train to Pau.

Chantel, the only woman in the group, started to give Francis a friendly lecture on how to act as a native, in English, until Francis started talking in his Pyrenean accent. This caused a great deal of laughter in the car and broke the ice. The others introduced themselves as Jean, and Phillipe, all young farmers of about the same age as Francis. They didn't seem to have been affected by the occupation yet.

Francis thought to himself, 'It's good not to be too serious as long as you are careful.' He decided that was how Jerry's luck had held.

During the trip of about two hours, Francis got to chat to Chantel as she was in the back with him. She quite fancied this good-looking young Frenchman sent from England to help the Resistance. She was telling him, 'You have to change at Toulouse.' She had the times of the trains from Poitiers, and they were trying to catch the 1.08. They were just on the outskirts of Poitiers when in Les Tebats, off the main road, there was a roadblock.

THE AUCTION ROOM

The Germans were being very officious and ordered them out of their car. Phillip (who had been driving) was tired and getting very cheesed off. So, Chantel took him around the back of the car to look at the rear tyre. Then in German, she asked one of the soldiers, who only looked about 16, to help, which surprised him. The other soldier asked to see Francis' papers. His papers were in the name of Paul Plurien from Toulouse. When the German soldier inspected his papers and then took them to show to his *Obergefreiter* (sergeant), Francis was a little nervous, as this was his first time of being questioned.

The second soldier was very aggressive and pushed his face against the side of their truck, demanding, '*Hände hoch, ruhig bleiben!*'

Just then, Chantel came with the other German soldier, chatting in his language. They carried on chatting for a while. Their papers were returned and the four of them piled back into the car. They were waved on with a smile for Chantel. His train was going to leave 25 minutes later, so Jean put his foot down. Francis had his ticket already, so he left the radio he had brought from England to deliver to them in the car with Phillip and ran for the train. He just jumped into the last carriage.

His adventure had started.

CHAPTER 10
William Parker's Story

HOLM FARM, PIXTON ESTATE,
SOMERSET, APRIL 1943-44

In 1943, Sandra Malone, a streetwise Liverpool lass who had volunteered as a land girl, was posted to the Pixton Estate. A very bright, strong, young 22-year-old, she had worked for several months helping broadcasting seeds for the following year's crop of wheat, and planting Mangelwurzel to be used as winter fodder. She was one of a group of 12 girls who shared very basic accommodation together. They were all from different parts of the country; some of them down to earth and some who felt that they were doing everyone a favour in getting their hands dirty. Being a scouser, she couldn't be doing with them. She had made friends with Linda, who was from Seahouses, Tyneside. They would give Fred Pickering Sergeant a hard time (he had been invalided out of active service) and posted as the organiser of the WLA in Dulverton. But he was not very good at organising women. His only way of controlling them was to pull rank and threaten them with dire consequences. Sandra had been sympathetic, but he mistook this for more than she intended. He fancied her and tried to get inside her knickers on several occasions, but Sandra was having none of it!

On Friday, she was in the hayloft moving bales and dropping them onto a hay wain in the yard. She didn't realise that Fred had come up the ladder behind her. Just as she swung around with the hay fork, he tried to grab her. As he put his arms around her to try to grab her breasts, he lost his footing and started to fall back down the hatchway headfirst. Still holding on to the fork, Sandra had speared him in the backside.

He fell into the hay below with the fork tines deeply embedded; the handle had broken off on the way down, moaning, 'Jesus! What did you do that for? Get the medic! Ooh Ah! Do something!'

Sandra was helpless; in fits of laughter, she dropped back into scouse. 'Ye' posh twat, meff bastard! You shouldn't have tried to get into my kacks! Yr' gobshite! Sit off and leave me alone.'

Fred shouted, 'Glad you think this is funny! Get this thing out of my arse and get me a medic. You are going to regret this, Miss Scouse!!'

Sandra, in tears of laughter, sat down and tried to recover.

Just then, Linda, her Geordie friend, walked in and saw Fred. Without thinking, she pulled the fork out of Fred's backside. Fred screamed and just lay there cursing, 'You bloody women!' threatening them with consequences.

Linda could see Sandra as she put her head down through the hatchway, streaming with tears of laughter. She came down the ladder, and they fell into each other's arms laughing, but Fred was not a happy bunny. He was pulling his trousers down, hopping about on one leg, trying to check his backside, and feeling it for blood.

The girls, trying to look concerned, took one look at Fred's backside and broke down again in uncontrollable laughter.

There was little or no sign of injury, but Fred was hopping about in pain. Just a little drop of blood appeared where each prong had entered; there was no apparent damage otherwise. At last, the girls realised that they had better help Fred put himself together; Linda ran out to find Joe Pooley (the farmer's son) for help. She couldn't find him, so they helped him put his trousers back on.

He had recovered enough to be very angry. He hobbled out and found his motorbike, and drove off, wobbling all over the place. Still trying to be serious, the girls came down to earth and wondered how he was going to get revenge for his hurt pride.

Linda, still laughing, said, 'I don't think he's going to report this. His ego is really injured more than his bum. He won't tell any of his oppos as they would really take the piss. But I reckon he'll find a way to get his own back. We'll get all the shit jobs. So, I think you should get in first and complain that he tried to corner you and tried to take advantage. I think his boss fancies you, anyway. If Lieutenant Granger, the good-looking Navy subbie in the wheelchair, takes your side, then Fred may be put on a charge or, with any luck, transferred. It's worth a try anyway!'

Fred didn't get transferred, but Lt Granger sent Sandra and Linda to work on the land in Brompton Regis. They were billeted to share the spare room at Pulhams Mill with Moira and Jerry. They settled into the routine of early mornings, but as it was getting dark earlier, now that winter was approaching, they would finish at 4.30 p.m. At weekends they would dress up and meet up with the other land girls from Pixton. There always seemed to be a dance.

The peace of Exmoor was shattered by dozens of large trucks bringing in American troops. Troop-carrying jeeps, artillery and small tanks were coming from all directions to Upton. They took over about 130 acres of land on the top of Haddon Hill, just to the west of the village of Upton. The How brothers and Cedrick Davey, the local agricultural engineers, were seconded to prepare the way. They were sworn to secrecy. They didn't really know why, exactly, or what was happening. The word had got around that there was a build-up of the American army within about 20–30 miles of the coast. It was obvious that there was going to be a big push against the Germans into France. The news was very minimal. People didn't talk about it. There was a general understanding that gossip could be picked up by fifth columnists and transmitted back to the enemy. But there was obviously something afoot.

All the local girls were very keen to go to the village hall dances to meet up with these good-looking lads from faraway places that they had never heard of. Because of rationing, the yanks' currency of stockings, chocolate, and all sorts of goodies that they had never seen before was very welcome. The local lads weren't very happy as they couldn't compete. Bill How's eldest, Gerald, was a very big, good-looking lad. He felt himself to be the most eligible and had always had the pick of the girls. He was a leading light in the young farmers. Over the years, Sandra Malone was the girl he considered to be 'his girl'. She didn't want to get stuck with a yokel at the moment, so she dumped him in favour of Staff Sergeant Bill Parker.

At the age of 20, William (Bill) was the youngest engineer training sergeant in the Engineering Regiment from Camp Chaffee, Arkansas, temporarily stationed in the newly constructed camp on Haddon Hill. Two hundred engineers and artillery troops had been shipped over from the US as part of a low-profile secret build-up of American troops in Devon and Somerset. Bill was among the hundreds of lads waiting to go to war with the Nazis.

The dances were organised by the welfare officer at the Britannica Camp for the lads to let off steam, and the regimental band had an off-shoot swing band. Although the locals had heard swing on the radio, they hadn't seen the dances. Word got around how great it was. It was so upbeat when all around there was doom and disaster. The band was in great demand in the village halls.

Dulverton town hall had a dance on Saturday night at 7 p.m. The Blue Band Swingers were billed to play. All the young local lads for miles around turned up. You didn't even have to pay to get in. All the land girls and the village girls whose parents would let them turned up.

(II)
PULHAMS MILL
SATURDAY 1 MAY 1944 AT 5 P.M.

There was great excitement at the Mill. The girls were dressing up and making do, doing their best with the limited makeup they had. They were drawing a seamline down their calves to make it look as if they were wearing stockings, and used charcoal for eye shadow. Moira had some lipstick, which was still available in London if you had lots of money. Her father had sent her assorted makeup from Harrods.

It was late spring, and there was a chill in the evening air, but it was dry, and the girls had a torch and were going to walk down Bury Hill to Dulverton. It would take about an hour to walk. Jerry offered them a lift on the tractor as Moira's Austin had a flat tyre.

Just as they were about to go, a jeep pulled up, and two GIs, Bill and Jedd jumped down. 'We'll take you to the dance,' they said. Linda fancied Bill's friend, Jedd, and the girls were up for it.

Jerry said, 'You had better bring them back before 11.30.'

'OK! No problem. I'm on early duty tomorrow, anyway. Are you their dad?'

'No! But I don't want to have to turn out at some ungodly hour to fetch them from Dulverton.' Then he added, 'Have you got any petrol you could let me have?'

'Yeah! I'll bring you a jerrycan tomorrow evening.'

Sandra had chatted to Bill Parker when he had been the driver for his CO, Major Joseph Blessing, who had come to Pixton Park to pay his respects to Lady Mary Herbert. Sandra really fancied him. With his southern US accent, he had asked her out, but she was playing hard to get.

The girls were excited and really wanted to go! They managed to climb aboard the jeep, and off they went. All four of them singing, 'Don't fence me in'. They had just heard it on the radio and were trying to sound like Bing Crosby and The Andrews Sisters.

(III)
DULVERTON TOWN HALL

They unloaded in Bank Square and ran up the stairs into the town hall. They were early, but the bar was open, and the band was just setting up. It was all set for a great night of swing, jitterbug, and bee bop; they took their drinks to a table to wait for it all to happen.

It was all too good to last. The doors swung open like in a Western movie. Three puffed-up young farmers arrived, trying to impress the girls, who just giggled. They made straight for the bar, looked threateningly at the GIs and pushed aside anyone in their way. Then the whole place suddenly filled up with excited, happy girls just wanting to have fun. The band started up, which broke the tension. The snare drum beat out the swing rhythm:

'Sing, Sing, Sing (with a Swing).'
Do-di-di-dedi-di,
Di-do-di-dd-id-it,
Di-dit-de-den,
Dedit-dodit-di-doti...

The trumpets, flugelhorn and trombones burst out in loud music. The band leader was singing and jitterbugging on the stage.

It looked as if it was going to be a good night! Bill gave Sandra some quick instructions on the basics of swing, and away they went. The atmosphere was really heating up as the GIs picked their partners, and the floor filled up.

A bloke in civvies came over and held out his hand to Laura, sitting next to Linda. As if they knew each other, they went to the centre of the floor. Wow! They could dance! The whole floor stopped to watch, forming a circle around a master class in swing!

Laura being tossed over the guy's head, then both holding on to each other's hands, their feet taping and gyrating fast, heel-toe* heel, toe* toe heel*toe*heel.

What would their feet do next?

He took her two hands and swung Laura between his legs and back again. then up over one shoulder, over back through his legs, then both standing. Hands over, hands cross over, change hands, facing each other, leaning back. Their feet were moving in time to the music * faster* faster.

Laura was being spun* pivoting on his hand, changing hands, two hands together, the guy going through her legs, sliding along the floor under and back.

Upright, standing*, pulling and lifting Laura high over his head, her legs straight out. Her dress spread like an umbrella, her legs apart as she landed on two feet* changing hands * to face each other, then turned* Beside each other, left toe out and back, right toe out and back, in unison!

The snare drum beat out the rhythm:

'Sing, Sing, Sing (with a Swing).'
Do-di-di-dedi-di,
Di-do-di-dd-id-it,
Di-dit-de-den,
Dedit-dodit-di-doti...

The trumpets and flugelhorns and trombones burst into play again as Barry Bywater took centre stage, then Frank on the double bass solo:

Boo-dob-di-bam-boo-di-bop
Bam-do-doo-bee-bee...

Laura and Co. kept on swinging and jitterbugging as the others broke the circle and joined in, and the whole floor erupted into the swing. Whirling dresses showed exciting glimpses of the girls' underwear.

To begin with, the older locals, who had come to watch their daughters, were tut-tutting! Then the mood caught them. The beat was irresistible. Their feet were tapping, and some were even starting to dance on the sidelines; the sound was so infectious. Only Gerald, Joe and Greg, the other young farmers, were wallflowers at the bar, still drinking. If looks could kill!

As Sandra swung past Gerald, he caught her arm and pulled her off the floor, shouting at the GIs, 'Rednecks, go home.'

Sandra bought her knee up as she spun around and caught him in the crotch (she said it was an accident!), but all the others cheered and laughed as Gerald crumpled to the floor! He had been made a fool of. This didn't bode well for the evening, but in the main, the mood stayed very hot and happy.

On the way out, to tend to his pride and his injured parts, Gerald pushed past Bill, spilling the drinks he was carrying. 'You're going to regret this, Yankee Doodle MOTHER FUCKER!'

Bill ignored him. He just went back to the bar, and Jedd topped up his warm beer and returned to the table with Sandra. Linda and Jedd were dancing close to a slow number. Bill and Sandra joined them. The floor was crowded, and as the night went on, the mood had changed to romantic.

Bill said, 'It's warm in here. Do you fancy a walk?'

Sandra replied, 'I hope Gerald's gone home, but I doubt it. We should go out the back way, through the fire escape. He thinks I'm his property; I hope you don't. I just want to have a good time. I like you! But we both know this isn't going to be long-term. You'll be gone soon. You're not going to get me pregnant. I'm a scouse, and we scouse girls don't take any nonsense from men.'

Bill said, 'OK, you win. I'm just a shy Yank. But you're really getting me turned on. I need to hold you. Let's get out of here.'

They stopped at the top of the fire escape, and Bill took her in his arms. His passion let loose! There was a ruckus going on in the high street.

Gerald said drunkenly, 'You Yanks thinking you can just walk into our country and take all our women,' taking a swing at a British Redcap who just pushed him, and he fell over. Sergeant Pickford (the local copper) was trying to keep the peace. He had to resort to getting help from the Redcaps. And then the US military police (the Red Bulls) arrived. This wasn't helpful!

The two forces found it hard to cooperate. It was very stupid. They each objected to the other arresting the other's soldiers. Gerald was a civilian, so there was almost an argument as to who should deal with him. Pickford knew Gerald, so he helped him up and marched him over to Joe and Greg, who were both in slightly better condition than Gerald. Gerald was still being a pain. Greg tried to restrain him, and he was being successful until he saw Brenda and Bill on the fire escape.

He staggered, lolloped over to the bottom step, and pulled himself up till he reached the landing. There, he took a swing at Bill, missed and overbalanced, falling backwards down the steps to the pavement and cracking his head on the curb. There was blood pouring from his head. Bill and Brenda rushed down to see if they could help.

Unfortunately, the posse of police didn't witness this as they'd gone to sort out an incident inside the hall.

Joe (who hadn't seen what had happened) said, 'You bloody Yanks. Your lot came over here to kill Jerries, not us. You won't get away with this.' He went to hit Bill, but Sandra dead-legged him, and he fell on top of Gerald. Bill was trying to pull him away from Gerald when the Redcaps returned. Greg accused Bill of murder.

They tried to arrest Bill after an argument with the US Red Bulls. Then Pickford came to see what was happening. They almost had a fight.

It just so happened that Major Joseph Blessing was giving Lady Foxton a lift home after a dinner party at

Pixton. He stopped when he saw that the US military police were involved in the incident.

'What's going on here?! We are guests in the UK, so sort this out. Why the argument?'

Sergeant O'Brien stood to attention. 'This man has been accused of murder, sir! The Limey police want to arrest him.'

'I don't care. Just clear the street! Bring him back to Britannica. We'll sort this out on home ground.'

'Yes, sir!!' He saluted.

The major swept away in his staff car.

Pickford said, 'I won't let the Red Bulls take this man. This is a crime in my jurisdiction.'

'That's a big word, Limey. He's ours, and we'll deal with him.'

All this time, Sandra was protesting Bill's innocence. 'You can't arrest a man on the word of that drunken, violent yokel scab. He didn't even see what happened.'

The US army ambulance arrived, and the medics were trying to resuscitate Gerald, but to no avail. They took him off to the US Military Hospital at Musgrove Park in Taunton.

Jerry arrived. He had the feeling that the GIs wouldn't have listened to him. He had managed to get the Austin back on the road. At first, he couldn't find them, but he followed the sound of an argument in Fore Street near the fire escape. He tapped Sandra on the shoulder.

'Where's Linda?'

'I don't know!' she sobbed. 'They can't take Bill. He was only protecting me, and he didn't even touch Gerald. He was drunk, overbalanced and fell down ten steps.' But she had reverted to scouse. So, no one there understood her.

'Calm down, Sandra.'

Linda appeared. 'Come on, Sandra. Let them sort it out. The Bizzies will arrest you if you make trouble.'

Sandra wasn't listening. She pounded the Red bull on the chest. He was taken aback by this raving girl attacking him (women in WaKeeney, Kansas, just wouldn't hit a man in public).

He caught hold of her hands and nearly broke her wrists.

This was getting out of control!

Pickford stepped in. 'Stop this now!' he commanded as reinforcements of Redcaps arrived with a lieutenant in charge. 'Stand down!' This broke the tension.

Bill had kept silent. He knew that it would be best to go back to his base. 'I will go back voluntarily. You don't have to cuff me! I'm sorry, Sandra. It was a great evening. These guys will look after me. I didn't do anything wrong. If I have to come to answer things, that's OK. The major will sort that out. Bye now. See you again. I don't think I'll be welcome in Dulverton anymore, though.'

Sandra, still crying, begged, 'Bill, please come and see me at the Mill.' She hung on his neck, kissing him.

Jedd reassured her, 'I'll make sure he's OK. The locals will be after his blood. It doesn't matter that the guy was drunk! This thing will calm down. Bill will have to leave soon; we all will anyway.'

The weather suddenly changed. It started to rain, and the wind was whipping around from the east. Soon it was turning to snow.

Bill and Jed were loaded into the jeep with the Red Bulls, and they were away!

Jerry tried to hug Sandra, but she pushed him away. 'Where's the tractor?' Linda took her to the Austin, and they loaded up.

Jerry said, 'We had better get up Bury Hill. I don't think this snow is going to stick, but you never know up here. We've had 6 inches of snow in June …

'I don't know! You girls! You seem to find trouble. Never mind, Pickford knows where you are. He knows about Gerald's violence and drinking. Gerald, Joe, and Greg! They're always having a go at the other locals who don't kowtow to them. I wouldn't say this to everyone, but Gerald had it coming to him. I've known him since he was four years old. He started drinking when he was 9. He wagged school in Brompton and would steal a tractor and scrumpy from his father's brew. He was likeable then, and he got away with murder. But he was hooked on cider and became very violent, particularly with his girlfriends. It was very strange because scrumpy usually befuddles the brain and makes people placid. But then, Gerald didn't have much of a brain!

'It's a shame that your evening was spoiled by those thugs. I wouldn't go near Joe and Greg. After what happened, they will be after Bill's blood, although they are both weak, just Gerald's followers.'

THE AUCTION ROOM

(IV)
SUNDAY 9.45 A.M.

US troops were doing their civic duty at a church parade. Several trucks went past the Mill.

Sandra, crossing to get some milk for breakfast, was almost run down. She saw Bill in his No. 1 uniform in the front of the lead truck, which screeched to a halt so that the following trucks nearly ran into the back of it. Bill jumped down and waved the others on. Sandra was in her slippers and dressing gown as it was her turn to have a lie-in. Linda was off to bring the cows in for milking.

Bill said, 'I can't stay long. Just wanted to say that I've just heard that Gerald isn't dead. When he arrived at Musgrove, they were just taking him to the morgue when he sat up! The medics nearly dropped the stretcher. He regained his mojo briefly but then collapsed again. They think he may have long-term problems. He won't be around for a while.'

Sandra ran to Bill and hung around his neck, her slippers falling off in the road.

'You've not been arrested? You'd better get on parade, or they will put you on a charge. I'll see you after the service at St Mary's. We could have a drink in The George, as long as Joe and Greg aren't there. I've got to help with the milking first.'

Bill carried her, arms still around his neck, and gently stood her on her feet on the porch. He kissed her full on the lips and doubled off. 'See you outside the pub,' he called.

She tiptoed barefoot on the cold track to pick up her slippers, still waving goodbye.

This was the last time Sandra was to see Bill alive.

(V)
WEST SOMERSET FREE PRESS - FRONTPAGE

Staff Sergeant Bill Parker was garrotted with a cheese wire on his way through the churchyard to take part in the parade, at St Mary's Parish Church, in Kings Brompton last Sunday. Two local men are being held for questioning. Sgt Pickford told us that he was not looking for anyone else in connection with this terrible crime against our friends and allies. We believe this was a grudge crime, which was based on a fight over a girlfriend and about an accident, which the protagonist thought was fatal. In fact, Gerald How survived a serious head injury from a fall of 16 feet from the fire escape of Dulverton Town Hall last Saturday at approx. 11 p.m. after a dance on the 1st of May.

If you witnessed either of these events, please come forward and call into Dulverton Police station or Telephone Dulverton 9333.

The suspicion was that Joe and Greg were waiting in the churchyard. Had they planned this? If they did, they were pretty stupid. How did they think they could get away with it? The local police were fairly slow, but this was so blatant that even the dimmest copper couldn't miss it. Actually, Pickford was a bright spark on his way to becoming an inspector.

(VI)
CHURCH PARADE OUTSIDE THE GEORGE PUB
SUNDAY 9 MAY AT 12.00 LUNCHTIME

All the GIs were on parade, and the brass band was playing their finale, 'Heaven's Gates Are Open Wide', as the congregation moved to the pub. The Reverend Greenway came running down the path, tripped and nearly knocked Sandra over in his panic to get to the band leader.

'Come quickly! One of your young men is lying dead near the sacristy door.'

The lieutenant in charge rushed up, and the sergeant-at-arms ordered, 'Attention! Parade, stand fast.'

The band kept on playing but changed to 'Abide with me'.

Then the realisation came to Sandra that the only GI that wasn't on parade was Bill! She ran up to the sacristy door but was stopped by Jerry, who had found Bill's body. He had come to check that there was no problem with Sandra from Joe and Greg.

He had challenged Greg as he was trying to disappear. There was no sign of Joe.

Sandra cried, 'It's Bill, isn't it? Is he OK? I must see him.'

Jerry, holding Sandra back, said, 'You can't do anything. He's gone.'

He held her as Moira arrived and guided her away. Sandra, sobbing, was having none of this. She broke away and dropped to her knees beside Bill, trying to bring him back to life. The Red Bulls arrived and dragged Sandra away back to Moira's arms.

Jedd shouted, 'What have they done? Those LIMEY BASTARDS! We're over here putting our lives on the line to defend them, and they're killing us. What's wrong with you all?'

Sergeant Pickford and Constable Brimblecombe moved the gathering crowd back. 'You can't move the body until the inspector arrives from Minehead. Back off and move away!'

The army medics argued, 'He's one of ours. You can't stop us.'

Major Blessing ordered, 'Let the sergeant do his job. I'm fed up with these arguments every time I come to church. Just stand down. We'll take Bill back when they have sorted out who did this.'

Sergeant Pickford said gratefully, 'Thank you, major. We will pull out all the stops and will keep you informed of our every move. We are trying to find the suspects. They are locals. Jerry here nearly caught one of them red-handed. We are very upset that these local thugs should have done this terrible thing to our allies. We need to sort this out so it doesn't get to be national news, as this might affect the war effort. Even the local press has been told to keep it low profile.

Sergeant Pickford used the phone box to call the inspector to get back up. He told Nigel all the details.

Brimblecombe of the Red Bulls said, 'We're standing by and waiting for the military ambulance to pick up Bill.'

Pickford was about to get on his bike, but the major called, 'Sergeant O'Brien, take Sergeant Pickford in the jeep to find these men. Use your pistol if necessary! He's in charge, OK. See you back at Britannica. Report your progress at 7.00 p.m.'

O'Brien saluted and jumped in the jeep with Sergeant Pickford.

'Where we are fixin' to-go, boss?'

'Just head to Britannica. Little Cowlings is on the way. Joe Cowling's probably not there, but it's a place to start.'

As they were headed past Pulhams Mill, Pickford couldn't believe his eyes. There was Gerald How (Just about alive) trying to break into the bungalow. They screeched to a halt.

'I thought you were dead. What are you doing here?'

'I might as well be. Me heads on fire!'

As he made a run for it, Joe Cowling came around the front and saw Pickford and tried to run, but O'Brien put his foot out and tripped him up, and he fell into

Pickford's arms. The policeman cuffed him to the iron railings.

'You think I killed Bill? It wasn't me. Greg and me were only going to rough him up a bit. We didn't know Gerald was alive. 'He's 'mazed as a rat…!'

Fred Cowling arrived then in his Land Rover.

'It's true. Frightened Betty to death. When I tried to stop him, he hit me in the stomach and doubled me up. He tried to find my shotgun, but it's safely locked up.'

'He's run down yonder t'wards Hickham.'

Pickford and O'Brien raced off in the jeep, through the river and across the fields after Gerald. His feet got stuck in the boggy hole. He released himself by pulling his feet out of his boots and ran on in his bare feet but snagged his toe on a rusty piece of barbed wire. He fell over, bleeding and cursing. As the jeep caught up with him, O'Brien (who played American football back home) tackled him. The jeep nearly turned over, but Pickford managed to get to the handbrake. This slewed it around, nearly turning it over into a ditch. It teetered on the edge and bounced back on all four wheels and stopped!

Gerald How was arrested and committed to the county assizes for garrotting Staff Sergeant Bill Parker of the US army. He was sentenced to hang, but his head injury from the fall caused him to have a stroke, and he died in Exeter Gaol while on remand.

CHAPTER 11

Jerry Winzor's Story – Part 4

THE MILL, 1945

Jerry and Moira lived at Pulhams Mill when the war was over, and when the SOE was taken back under the wing of MI 5/6, the male-dominated organisation took back the important posts from women.

And Moira was to be demoted. BB was not happy that Moira had made such a success as the head of his establishment at Venne. Moira didn't relish working for the department anymore, but for the time being, she was still employed and had staff that were doing important work related to the Soviet Union. Her job was not really defined. She had administration to do, but after the drama of wartime SOE, it was dull. She did feel pangs of guilt, having sent young women into occupied France who never returned! That was her job! She had made friends with them all and tried her best to give them the tools to survive.

Her father didn't want his daughter to have 'anything to do with this criminal, Jerry Winzor', but Moira had independent means. Her grandfather, Lord Berkeley, had left her a property in Cambridge Square, London W1, which was looked after by his solicitor. It had survived the Blitz in reasonable condition. It was a 5-storey building with the Belfrance Restaurant on the ground and first floors. In the basement was a nightclub called Bungy's and there were three flats above. The rents were substantial, and Moira had the top flat as her pied-à-terre, so, much to her father's (now Sir David Pemberton) dislike of her relationship, he couldn't stop it. He did try!

One Saturday morning, as Jerry was sitting in the tin bath in the bungalow kitchen, and Moira, being a proper country girl, was scrubbing his back and singing, 'Widecombe Fair', two burly policemen barged in the unlocked door.

'We're here to arrest Jerry Winzor.'

Moira still had her SOE identity card in the pocket of her riding britches (she had just returned after an early morning ride). 'Who the hell do you think you are, barging into the house of a government official?'

Sergeant Pollard said, 'We have instructions from Inspector Birch to arrest this man, Winzor.'

Moira retorted, 'To start with, how do you even know if you have him here? Have you got a record of his birthmarks?'

They backed off and stood looking like naughty schoolboys.

Moira produced her MI6 identity card. They tried to make excuses, but Moira was having none of this! 'Leave at once and report back to London that Jerry Windsor is part of my team. I will take any flack Birch might throw this way.'

Jerry was just being his usual relaxed self, sitting naked in the bath, smiling while all hell let loose around him. 'If you can't do anything about it, relax!'

Both cops scurried out with their tails between their legs!

Moira returned from seeing them off the premises.

'I don't know how you do it! Just sailing through life! This must be the reason I love you!'

(II)
PULHAMS MILL, NOVEMBER 1946

Time went on. The two of them were happy living as subsistence farmers. Moira had matured into a tall and portly farmer's wife, and Jerry had settled back into his boyhood as a farmer. They had about 25 cows, which they milked with the compressor that Bertie had left when he moved into the village.

The winds were coming from the east, which was very unusual. The prevailing winds on Exmoor are usually from the west. There was a definite chill as winter approached fast. Pulhams Mill was very sheltered under the lee of a north hill and facing south. Even in January, Moira and Jerry could sit out at the front on an afternoon when the sun was out, but it seemed as if this was going to be a hard winter.

The village didn't know much about Venne, and since the beginning of the war, the locals had accepted males and females living in the same house as a necessity of the war, but the vicar, the Reverend Greenway, was trying to lift the morals of his parish. He would visit Moira and Jerry and try to convince them that they should get married.

Moira quite liked the idea, and Jerry was moving in that direction. Moira's father was so opposed to it that he even came down just before Christmas, not to celebrate, but to try to take Moira back to London. It was he who had tried to get Jerry arrested, but it hadn't worked. He thought that if he was to make trouble for Jerry in the village, he might convince his daughter that he was no good, and she would return to London with him. His grand plan was going to turn into worms.

The day he arrived, and it started to snow. It seemed it was going to be a white Christmas. At the time, he rolled up in an ancient Woolsey taxi, both Jerry and Moira were helping Fred Cowling about 3 miles away, so David was dropped outside the bungalow, and he had to wait for them to return. It was naughty of Bill Buckley to leave him outside in the snow, but he didn't like incomers. It was about an hour before they returned, and David was not dressed for the country. He was very cold and very cheesed off when they finally came back.

Moira thought it was a snowman standing outside, shivering. 'Why didn't you go inside? We never lock the door. Come in and dry off in front of the Rayburn. Father, you must take off that coat. It's soaked through. You'll catch your death.'

Jerry rallied around, stoking the fire and putting the kettle on for a hot drink.

'Moira! What do you want to do, living in a godforsaken hole like this when you have a flat in town? It's 10° warmer in London. Your mother would have been ashamed of you, living in sin with this reprobate. What do you imagine your sister thinks? She'd like to come and see you with her daughter, but she doesn't feel safe with you living with an attempted rapist.'

Moira was trying not to lose her temper with her father. She knew that he just wanted the best for her. He was also still grieving for her brother, who had been lost at sea when his destroyer had been sunk by a torpedo. He was a hero who had been destined to follow in David's footsteps as a surgeon. He had studied at Guy's Hospital to be a specialist. Much against his father's wishes, he had joined the Navy as a medic to help in the war effort.

Jerry tried to keep out of this family issue. He felt that he wanted to pour oil on troubled waters. For the time being, he held his peace.

Moira sat down beside her father and put her arms around him. They had always had a good relationship. She was hoping that when he warmed up and calmed down, they could have a sensible chat and resolve some of the issues.

The snow continued to fall, and it was settling; by that evening, it would be at least 6 or 8 inches deep.

Sir David had come to take his daughter back to London, and he was determined that he would catch the train from Dulverton, to change in Taunton and catch the 6 p.m. to Paddington.

Moira gave him lunch: a hot lamb stew with dumplings. The three of them sat in silence and ate. Jerry offered him some of his stash of brandy.

David refused it, saying, 'I don't want anything from you! You probably stole it anyway.'

'Don't be ridiculous, Dad. I bought that because I know you like a drop now and again.'

'Don't call me "Dad". You know I don't like it. You're becoming influenced by this renegade.'

When he had eaten, he stomped out to the lounge, picked up the phone and tried to call a taxi. They said they would attempt to get up to the Mill, but the snow was thick. They would attempt Bury Hill, but if they didn't get there in an hour, that would mean that they wouldn't be coming. It was getting to be too late, but he felt if he started walking, he could still catch the train.

Moira gave him a waxed jacket, and she started walking with him just as they met the taxi. Sir David tried to convince Moira to get in the taxi with him.

'No, Dad. I still work here.'

'Never mind about that; I'll sort it out with Bolsover.'

'What is your problem? I think you had better just go back to London, and I will come up and visit you when I can get away. I'm trying to keep this whole thing civil, but if you can't see that, then I don't know what else I can do. I am certainly not going to leave a perfectly good relationship just because you don't like Jerry. He may have been a bad boy once, but he is good for me! Just get in the taxi and go before you get stuck here for months. This snow is getting deeper by the moment.'

Moira waved her father goodbye.

When she returned to the Mill, Jerry was digging out the path to the shippen. Before the snow was too deep, he called the cows down to the gate and fetched them into the shelter. The ten Exmoor Horn sheep were happily under the lee of a hedge, but he took some grain nuts and made sure the water trough was filling. It would probably freeze that night, so he took some fleece waste and wrapped the water pipe to keep it warm. He would have to come and sort it out in the morning to defrost it.

Then they hunkered down. Fred Cowling (a local old-timer) reckoned the signs were that this was going to be the hardest winter in a hundred years. Jerry decided to get on the tractor and go down to Dulverton to get more feed for the next months and buy some more flour and paraffin for the Tilley lamp. They had a shed full of logs for the Rayburn. On the way down Bury Hill, he was slipping and sliding about. He went as fast as he could, but he missed the fact that the taxi had swerved off the road because the skid marks had been covered already. The taxi was in a field; it had turned over, but it had already been covered in snow.

It wasn't until he was on the way back up the hill that he saw it. He nosed the tractor through an open gate and went as far as he could to get as close to the taxi as possible. The snow was very deep, and the tractor was slipping sideways downhill, but he managed to slew the tractor uphill again. He could see two people apparently unconscious inside. He left the tractor running and scooped the snow from the passenger's side, and managed to open the front door enough to see if there was any sign of life. The engine was still running, and he could smell petrol. He decided to try to pull David out. He seemed to be conscious but very groggy. He pulled him clear of the car and was trying to get Bill out of the other door when there was an explosion. Jerry had his head and shoulders inside. The force turned the vehicle over, and it rolled down the hill, crushing Jerry and breaking his neck. He died instantly.

Jerry's Luck had run out!

Sir David regained consciousness and managed to climb away from the burning wreck. He wasn't totally aware of what had happened, but he realised that whoever was in or near the taxi would have died. Still, being a doctor, his instinct was to go and try to rescue any survivors. He tumbled down the hill towards it, but as he got closer, he saw that there was no chance anyone could still be alive. He was still in a daze as he tried to go for help.

Cedric Vaisey was driving his sheep down the next-door field and heard and saw the flames and the explosion. He made his way over the stile and could see Sir David struggling uphill. When he reached him, David collapsed but asked to be taken to his daughter.

'They're all dead in the taxi!'

'Where's your daughter?'

'The Mill.'

'Which mill?'

'PULHAMS!'

Cedric (a very big, strong farmer) picked up David and put him in Jerry's tractor, which was still running. He made slow progress but covered the four miles in about an hour. As he was moving up the hill, he looked back and could see more vehicles on the bottom road; figures trying to put the fire out.

Moira came out into a blizzard. She thought that it was Jerry returning. As she reached the tractor, she could see it was Cedric and her father.

'Where's Jerry? What's happened?'

Cedric carried Sir David inside and laid him on the couch.

David said, 'He pulled me out of the car and went back for the driver and then it went up! I'm sorry, Moira. He's gone! He's a hero. I'm so sorry!'

Moira, really out of character, just burst into tears. All the drama of the loss of her husband and the loss of Jerry, the loss of all the brave people whom she had sent back to France over the past terrible war years, caught up with her at that moment.

Her father and she were reunited at that moment.

Jerry Winzor had made his last act of contrition.

The snow was so deep and frozen hard. It was three months before Sir David and Moira could get back to London. So, they made the best of the facilities at the Mill, and Sir David became a countryman for the duration.

The Venne facility was eventually closed. Some of the staff were transferred to Whitehall, as was Moira, who decided to resign and return to London with her father.

Pulhams Mill was left to go back to God.

The Spirits of the Mill liked Moira and Jerry.

Now they were getting very lonely. They did like company but were very choosy. They would be happy if Francis returned.

CHAPTER 12
Francis Pestone's Story

FRANCE, MAY 1944

After having jumped onto the train in Poitiers, he went to sleep until he was rudely awakened by the ticket collector with a German soldier checking papers. Francis had nothing to worry about as he was a French native, and he used his real name and papers as he was heading home. The German gave a cursory glance at his papers. But he questioned him through the ticket collector. Francis said that he had been to visit his cousin's ex-wife in Cahors, which was very close to the truth. He changed trains in Toulouse and had to wait for an hour for the connection. While he was waiting and snoozing on the platform, Jean-Baptiste sat down beside him, almost frightening him to death. Jean-Baptiste hugged Francis. He said that for the time being, he should go home to Buziet and lie low as a 'sleeper'.

Francis carried on farming with his cousin. His Aunt Sarah was having her second child, so the neighbour's daughter, Charlotte, was still helping on the farm. She hadn't married and was still smitten with Francis. When they met again, Francis remembered how much he needed the loving hand to soothe the pain of the loss of his mother. She took Francis in her arms, and there was no doubt that this was what they both wanted. He wanted to follow in Jerry's footsteps and work against the occupying forces in his country, but he had too many issues of his own. By having a radio to communicate with the SOE, he worked with Jean-Baptiste but realised that if he operated in the field, he would not last five minutes! Francis settled down and worked on at the farm with his cousin.

Francis and Charlotte were married in a very quiet wedding in Arudy. Her sister, Silvia, and Jean-Baptiste were witnesses. Life went on at the farm as it had for centuries.

The farm became a meeting place for active members of their Resistance group. In 1944 it was a very useful resting place for the British and Charles de Gaulle's Free France Army that was moving from the south, connecting with the Americans coming from the Atlantic coast.

(II)
PESTONE'S FARM, BUZIET NEAR ARUDY, 1955

Charlotte had always wanted to go to England. She had reached a very good standard of English at night school in Pau. It had been difficult during the war because the Germans tried to ban all languages except German. Because Francis was bilingual, they would speak in English when they were out on the farm.

It was quite possible for them to leave the farm with Bernard, who had met up with Charlotte's younger sister, Silvia. Bernard was really happy to run the farm. His wife didn't want anything to do with him, and when they could, Bernard and Silvia were planning to get married. So, Charlotte and Francis decided they would go to England.

They took a ferry from Bordeaux to Plymouth. The Mill was in a sorry state. The bungalow was in need of a lot of TLC. It was eight years since Moira had left. The asbestos roof tiles were still in good condition, so the building was dry. There had been a burst pipe in the bad winter of 1947, but, luckily, the water had frozen so that when it defrosted, it ran out of the front door and didn't do any harm to the structure.

Charlotte was happy to make a home for her and Francis there. Francis had come back to where he was born. At first, they stayed in Broom Cottage with Bertie and Joyce in the spare room. They had soon painted and cleaned the bungalow inside and out, and by the end of a week, the place was looking good. There was plenty of second-hand furniture. The Carnarvons were renovating three of the cottages on the Pixton Estate and auctioning them off at the monthly sale in Dulverton Town Hall.

Charlotte was getting to know the locals. Her English was not that good, but people were enchanted by her accent. She looked like a younger version of Eloise, Francis' mother. They had been very sad that she had left under such a cloud, although Francis didn't let them know about the terrible tragedy. Jerry had outlined that it was a hunting accident. Everyone who heard the story was appalled. To shoot your own mother is a nightmare!

There was a lot of residual support for the French after the terrible German occupation of France, but no one said anything to Francis or Charlotte.

Joyce was being very careful about what to say to Charlotte, who was aware of her treading on eggshells. She felt that she should explain to her that she knew the details of Eloise's death. Francis had told her before they married. She said, 'Please don't make Francis more aware of his guilt by making him feel that you pity him. I know you care for him as you have known him since birth, and he loves you because you saved him from Jerry. You probably don't understand how he could come to even talk to Jerry.'

Charlotte was trying in her second language to say the right things to explain this very delicate problem.

'The thing is that Jerry Winzor was genuinely in love with Eloise. The war had brought them together, and Jerry followed Eloise to the Pyrenees. The occupation and his experience in fighting with the Resistance had a cathartic effect on him. When they met, they were somehow destined to be together. The death of Eloise tied Jerry and Francis in a bond of shared grief.'

Joyce needed to know all this and was in tears. 'Thank you for telling me the real story! You know what villages are like. Someone cuts their finger, and by the time it gets to the other end of the village, they've lost a leg!'

She put her arms around Charlotte and pulled her to her motherly breast. Charlotte started to cry as she missed her mother's hugs; their family were very tactile.

'I think you should be straight with Francis. Although he will never get over the loss of his mother, he has come to terms with it, and he does love and respect you.'

'I think he would like to talk to somebody who knew Eloise. He knew that you cared for his mother.'

Charlotte had come to see Bertie to borrow his tractor and trailer to collect the furniture that they had bought at the auction in Dulverton.

Just as Joyce and Charlotte had dried their eyes, Bertie's timing was immaculate; he walked into the kitchen for his lunch. He took his boots off and said hello! He put his arm around Charlotte's shoulders and gave her a fatherly hug. He was ready for his food. Joyce was stirring the lamb stew and asked Charlotte if she would like some. She said she would take some stew back down to the Mill as Francis was painting the second bedroom; he was preparing it for the good news that they were expecting their first child. Both Joyce and Bertie were overjoyed for them.

Charlotte and Francis were happy at the Mill, and some months later, their daughter, Eloise, was born in Minehead Hospital. She was their pride and joy. She was christened in St Marys, and at the age of five, she attended the village school.

Mrs Steer was the new teacher who had been appointed, and she was a local. She had taught in Minehead but had always wanted to return to her roots and teach in the village school that she had attended until she won a place in Taunton School and, later, the university in Exeter.

Charlotte and Francis decided to return to France as Francis' sister wasn't well, and his cousin was going back to Cahors to look after his children.

Church Cottage

CHAPTER 13
Fran and Peter's Story

PULHAMS MILL, NOVEMBER 1978

The bungalow at the Mill had been empty for about four years. It was looking very sad. The fact that there had been no one living there meant that the rats had moved in and the woodwork was very tatty. The roof was sound, so it wasn't damp, but it was in great need of modernising as it had no bathroom. To bathe it was necessary to fill up the tin bath in front of the Rayburn.

In times gone by the Rayburn had been a luxury. It was good to have it as it did heat the water and was the heart of the house.

Peter and Fran Phillips had come to the UK on holiday from Australia. They had been running a restaurant in Paddington in Sydney. Peter's sister had a cottage in Huish Champflower about nine miles from Brompton Regis and they stayed there while they were looking for a place to buy in the UK so that when they came on holiday, they would have a place to stay. They still had their business in Paddington, Sydney.

The Spirits liked them.

The Mill was very cheap, but by then, it had turned into a 'romantic ruin'. There was nothing left of the mill machinery, the leat was overgrown, and the mill pond had large trees growing in it. The stone wall water retainer had almost disappeared and was overgrown with ivy. The wooden waterwheel had been broken up for firewood 65 years before.

I wouldn't say Fran and Peter fell in love with the Mill. They just seemed to be destined to take it on and rebuild it. I suppose it was a big challenge for Peter. They originally thought they could get a few local tradesmen to make it liveable, and then it would be a place they could come over to from Australia before returning home to Sydney again.

They couldn't live there as the Mill needed a lot of things done to it. They bought a caravan from Ross Billings, their architect. He was living on the other side of

THE AUCTION ROOM

Wimbleball Lake (actually, it is a reservoir, but they couldn't spell 'reservoir', so they called it a lake). No one knows where the name came from!

The idea was to live in the caravan while the work was underway. Then they would drive over in the morning and try to make the bungalow liveable. There was the Rayburn and an open fire.

Fran couldn't stand the wallpaper. 'Let's paint the whole place white,' she suggested.

It was early November when the sale was completed. Although the weather was cold, it was fine. This was an adventure. It was a long time since Fran had experienced a winter with snow as she had been taken out to Australia at the age of nine with her parents as a 10 lb-Pom. They were warm in the cottage in Huish as it had good heating, which was more than could be said for the Mill.

The shortcut to the mill was through Cuckoo's Combe. It was getting icy, so they would have to go the long way back. When the sun went down, the temperature would drop, and the road through Cuckoo's Combe would be dangerous. It was all very exciting to have a real winter! In Sydney, they only had to use the one-bar electric fire to keep warm, and then only for a day or two in July.

They bought some logs and kindling and lit the Rayburn. It was warming up, and Fran said, 'It's nearly 11 o'clock. I'll put the kettle on and make tea.'

Peter said, 'I'll get the paint out of the Daf.'

They did well, and by 3.30 p.m., they had painted three rooms white.

Peter said, 'That looks great. I think we can have an 'early mark' and go back to Huish before it gets dark.'

It was a long time since Peter had driven in winter. The roads on the way back were icy, but they arrived in Huish in one piece.

The next day was Saturday. It was sunny and dry, so they went past the Mill to Dulverton to pick up a Tilley lamp, paraffin, and some food for the weekend, and then it was back to the Mill to do some more painting.

They walked in. What had happened? The paint they had put on yesterday was lying in great white sheets on the floor. Fran, almost in tears, cried, 'All our hard work is on the floor. How did that happen?'

Peter said, 'The water in the emulsion paint must have frozen. No point in doing it again until the weather improves.'

It looked very much as if it was going to snow. The best thing was to just pack up and go, so they went back to Huish. They were unable to return for three months.

(II)
CHURCH COTTAGE, HUISH CHAMPFLOWER, NOVEMBER 1978

By the time they reached the cottage, the snow was 6 inches deep. Peter's sister, Jenny, had sorted a load of logs before she went back to join her husband, Mitchell, in the Caribbean. The heating was from a solid fuel Rayburn, so Peter and Fran would be warm even if they lost power.

It snowed all night and the next day. They woke on a Sunday at 9 a.m., and the sun was shining, and the air was crystal clear. The vicar, the Rev. Kev, couldn't get to the church and started to dig a path, but he was fighting a losing battle. The sides of the path kept falling in.

Fran was very excited. 'It's a fairyland. We have to go for a walk. Come on! I want to build a snowman.'

It was so different to Sydney. Fran had been nine years old when her parents emigrated to Australia. Six weeks on *The Fairsea* to a completely new world; she didn't want to go. She loved the English countryside.

Ten years before, Peter had done an overland trip through France, Germany, Austria, Communist Yugoslavia, Greece, Turkey, Afghanistan, Pakistan, India, Thailand, Malaysia, Singapore, Indonesia, Timor, Darwin, Catherine, and Longreach in Australia, finally arriving in Paddington, Sydney.

Fran was working in an art studio with a 'blond bombshell', Helen, who was going out with Peter. But Helen was looking for a rich man who would keep her in the manner to which she felt she was entitled; Peter was not that man. Rather than just dumping him, she introduced him to Fran. This was fairly perceptive of Helen.

This relationship was to last. Fran and Peter Phillips became a long-term item. They went into business together and started a restaurant in Five Ways but living on Hollingsworth Street in Paddington. Peter and a friend renovated the terrace. Peter had been working as an electrician in London, so he could do the wiring.

Wanting to be creative, he started making furniture and became a very accomplished craftsman. They also ran the Ça Va French restaurant with Beatrix Poitère for five years. Then Fran and Beatrix put a recipe book together that was a big success. In the top ten! They sold 20,000 copies in the first year and made enough money for Fran and Peter to go on an extended holiday to find a place in the UK with the thought that they might buy a run-down place and maybe sell the business in Sydney and stay in the UK. They left Beatrix in charge. She was happy to run the restaurant her way and she would be happy to buy Peter and Fran's share.

(III)
BACK AT CHURCH COTTAGE

Peter opened the side door of Church Cottage and discovered 4 feet of snow. He had prepared. The spade was leaning against the door that fell in. He spent the next two hours digging a path. It was worth it. By the time he had finished, he was really warm. This weather suited him. Fran followed him out. As she passed him, Peter put a handful of snow down the back of her neck.

Fran screamed, 'You won't get away with that!' and Peter ran off with Fran in hot pursuit. He slipped as Fran slid into him. They ended up in a heap covered in snow. Next door's dog was barking and was really enjoying this, dancing from foot to foot. Five-year-old Jill and her big brother, Bill, came out to join in the fun. A snowball fight ensued. Big flakes of snow started to fall, and they were all covered.

Fran went in to put the mince pies in the oven and make a hot toddy for Brian and Judy and hot juice for their kids. By 4 p.m., as the sun went down, the temperature dropped, and the snow was getting very deep. The Brents only just managed to get home next door. Everyone hunkered down for the night. The Rayburn was pushing out the heat. Peter lit the log fire and was hanging the Christmas decorations up that Fran had had the forethought to buy when they were on special in Pincombe's Hardware at Wiveliscombe. Peter had asked the guy behind the counter if he knew of any local builders who could help with the renovations at the Mill. Frank suggested Chris Lawrence. 'He's a great worker. He's usually in the Castle Pub in Huish on Tuesday nights for darts.'

The best thing to do for a couple of days was to just sit tight and stay warm. The snow kept falling, but they had plenty of food and logs. The TV wasn't working, so they listened to Radio 4. They were becoming addicted to the afternoon play. On Saturday at 11 a.m. there was *The Hitchhiker's Guide to the Galaxy*. They felt that radio was better than TV as you could imagine the pictures in your head.

Eventually, after a week, Peter was getting stir-crazy. The snow had stopped, so they started to dig themselves out. The sun came out, and the snow started to melt. Peter's Uncle Andrew (not really an uncle but a

THE SPIRITS OF PULHAMS MILL

very old family friend of his mother) had found the Daf motor car for them when they arrived in the UK. It was cheap to buy and run. It also had a form of limited slip differential that made it good on ice and snow. At the moment, the snow was so deep that the Daf had disappeared completely under it.

Tuesday afternoon.

Fran and Peter set about clearing a pathway so they could walk up to The Castle pub. The snow had melted in the sun during the morning, but by 3 p.m., the sun had moved behind the hill to the west, and the temperature dropped dramatically. The snow was freezing as they dug. It was turning into ice. This was getting to be hard work. As they were getting exhausted, their neighbour, Den, was trying to walk by, with great difficulty, using a spade as a walking stick.

'Yer! I think you need some help. This damn snow ain't going to stop any time soon! They say 'tis going to go on for another month at least. Have you got enough logs and food?'

Peter replied, 'I think we're OK at the moment, but we could really do with some help with this. I don't think we've met. I'm Peter, and this is Fran. I expect you know my sister, Jennifer. She's away in the Caribbean. I bet they're nice and warm there. You're Den? Thanks.'

With the three of them, it took about three-quarters of an hour to dig their way to The Castle. Johnathon, the publican, had a hot chocolate waiting for them when they reached the bar door.

Den said, 'I'd rather have a brandy, John.'

'You can have one tonight, but I'm afraid you'll have to pay for it.'

'Never mind, that'll do. It'll warm the cockles. Thanks. See you tonight for the darts match. I doubt if Skilgate'll get here! Still, we can have a practice and a laugh.'

Surprisingly, when Fran and Peter arrived at the pub at 7.30 p.m., the bar was full. Locals had trudged through a blizzard to get there. Peter recognised Chris Giddings, an antiques dealer, who arrived with 18-inch squares of hardboard tied to his feet with bailer twine as snowshoes. The gathering couldn't believe it. He took off his army greatcoat and produced a roll of £50 notes. 'Had to walk on top of the hedges. The snow was that deep, there were places where I could touch the telephone wires. The drinks are on me!'

The whole bar was in shock.

Peter said, 'You must have won the lottery.'

'No! it's my Christmas tradition. It's the only time I buy these buggers a drink. If I didn't, I'd be barred from the pub. For my sins, this is the nearest pub to Huddford Farm.'

Peter said, 'Thanks. I'll have a pint of Ushers. Fran, what'll you have?'

Fran replied, 'It's very kind of you. I'll have a house white wine. Can you introduce us to Chis Lawrence?'

Chris (a gentle giant of a guy: 6-foot tall, bushy beard) was standing behind them at the bar waiting to get a pint of Guinness, talking in a very high pitch to his local friends in local dialect (which was almost a different language).

'Tis I.'

Peter said, 'I think you did some work for my sister in Church Cottage?'

Chris offered his hand, which was like a giant's compared to Peter's. His handshake was crushing.

'Yes, 'twas me that done 'er kitchen a year since.'

Peter asked, 'Do you know Pulhams Mill at Brompton Regis? We've just completed on the sale. You were recommended by Frank in Pincombe's as the man who could help me. There is a lot of work needs doing there. Still, I don't think we could get there at the moment.'

Chis replied, 'In the next days, maybe a month. I'm on my ol' John Deere clearing them lanes! Anyhow, no way you'n get along till them lanes is cleared.'

Peter asked, 'What's a John Deere?'

Chis, chuckling, explained, 'It's a track bulldozer. This snow is packed. It needs tracks to get along. Be glad to have the work. I've worn out two sets of tracks already.'

Peter told him, 'There is a lot to do at the Mill. We're going to knock down the bungalow. Then there is a septic tank to put in and rebuild the Mill. It's only one and a half storeys at the moment. It must have lost its roof at some stage. The stone wall must have crumbled before they put on the corrugated. If they hadn't done that, the whole place would have fallen down.'

Chris said, 'You should have a word wi' Den Courtney. He got Betty up along Ol' Davies' daughter from Kings Brompton. Heya, Den. Meet the people who've just bought Pulhams Mill.'

Den laughed and said, 'I just helped them clear the way to the pub. Lewis Steer took the waterwheel out of the mill 60 year since. He used it for firewood. He sold it to the villagers. Cos 'twas elm. Him don't burn. Elm wood wet or elm wood dry burns like churchyard mould. E'n the flames is cold. Them wanted their money back. So, he was in real trouble as he'd spent the money in The George.'

Den (the one-eyed digger driver) worked for Chris. He was famous for losing his eye (on Guy Fawkes Night years ago when a stray firework had hit him).

Peter bought a round of drinks, and then Fran wanted to go home and get some supper.

Chris said, 'I'll call in at Church Cottage with some logs tomorrow. Only £10.'

Peter said, 'Great! See you then. We're going home to put some logs on the Rayburn now and hunker down for the night.'

The weather worsened overnight. Not only was it snowing, but the wind was howling around the church, but the cottage was protected from the worst of the wind by the church. The snow was building up against the doors. At the front, it was halfway up the windows.

They were warm and cosy inside. A stray ginger tom had wandered in a couple of days ago, and they had named him Mr Treacle. Fran fed him, and so he made himself at home. This was the first real winter Fran had seen in 25 years. They were happy just reading and listening to the radio.

Chris couldn't get to Church Cottage, although he did phone to check that Fran and Peter were OK.

He would make it when he could get his John Deere started. The battery was flat, and he had to dig his way to the shed to start the generator. There was a problem; it should have started automatically. He needed it, anyway, to run the house lights.

(IV)
CHURCH COTTAGE, 20 DECEMBER

Although the weather had improved, there was no way that Peter and Fran could get to the Mill, although they had managed to get to Wiveliscombe and eventually to Taunton to do some Christmas shopping. They did try to get to the Mill via Dulverton, but the town was completely cut off. There was a gathering, an army of diggers and track machines trying to clear roads. The snow had become so impacted that it was like concrete.

They had a very quiet Christmas. Jennifer rang from the Caribbean. They had bought a sailing boat. They crewed it and chartered it out. Mitchell was flying Dakotas for Virgin Islands Airways, but he had a fair amount of downtime. They enjoyed sailing round the islands, but Christmas wasn't the same! Their daughter, Alexia, would be coming back to England for the beginning of the new term at St Audrie's boarding school in late January. Peter would pick her up from Heathrow and drive her to Quantock's Head.

THE AUCTION ROOM

(V)
PULHAMS MILL, LATE JANUARY

At long last, Fran and Peter managed to get to the Mill.

Chris gave Peter a lift on his John Deere. It was a very cold and uncomfortable ride, but Peter had bought a Navy greatcoat, so he survived.

He thought to himself, 'These locals are tough.' Chris only had overalls and a padded shirt.

Fran followed in the Daf. Chris had a look around the Mill to see what he was taking on. There was a lot of stonework, but Chris was a can-do country lad. 'No problem.'

Peter said, 'We'll pay for your time, and we'll buy the materials from Pincombe's; they're local and seem to be the best builders' merchant around.' Plus, Chris had gone to school with most of the blokes that worked there.

Chris and Den started work in late February. The old Mill was built into the 20-foot mort slate cliff (known locally as shillet). The first thing was to separate the stone building from the cliff. This immediately cured the damp problem. The next big job was to dig a 15-foot-deep hole, which kept filling up with water (it was below the level of the river). It had to be that deep so that they could get a 1 in 64 runoff for the drains to stretch to the 1200-gallon fibreglass septic tank that looked like an over-size giant round-bottomed scientific flask.

The random stone wall building was going well.

Chris would sing hymns as he worked; a real country lad: if he picked up any random stone, it would always fit perfectly. This is a very special skill. As a result, he worked very quickly. Chris and Den worked as a team. Chris always had a problem with his vehicles. He bought most of them from his 'scrappy' friend Jeff, and they would only ever last a couple of months.

Peter had bought a new Toyota pickup. He said Chris could have the Daf. He was going to pay for it eventually, but the main thing was to keep Chris and Den working, so the payment went on the back burner for now.

(VI)
HUISH CHAMPFLOWER, 8.30 A.M.

Chris was to pick Den up from his council house one frosty, misty morning. There was a problem with the Daf's fuel pump (make do and mend, that's what country people did). The pump was no good, so he used a 1-litre petrol tank from a lawnmower tied to the top of the engine to gravity feed the fuel. Surprisingly, that worked OK.

Chris left it to run while he went up the steps. As Den opened his front door, they both looked back down the path and couldn't work out what the misty glow was. As they went down the steps, they felt a raging heat from the Daf, which had burst into flames! Nothing fazed Chris. He just got on with it. Peter and Fran had to laugh; no one had been hurt. They had already written off the Daf anyway.

THE AUCTION ROOM

(VII)
PULHAMS MILL

The weather had improved. But it wasn't finished with them yet.

One Sunday in May, Peter was happily soaking in his newly installed bath in what had once been the old larder in the bungalow when the snow started to fall. Peter was wallowing in luxury when he realised that the glazier had not arrived the previous day. There was no glass in the windows of the Mill. The new oak floors would be getting soaked! They might expand and crawl up the walls. All his work would be ruined.

Peter, in his dressing gown and slippers, joined Fran frantically trying to staple sheets of plastic instead of glass. Almost as soon as they had finished, it stopped snowing. That's life!

By June, they had weatherproofed the original half of the rebuilt Mill and moved in. Ross, the architect, helped knock down half of the bungalow, ready for the new build of the second half on the old bedrock foundations.

Chris and Den really 'got their fingers out.' The last thing to be installed in the carpet room, under the stone arch, was the Art Deco arched glass door saved from the bungalow. Chris had used the arched frame as a template. This was to be the entrance to the tea rooms in about 20 years' time.

It wasn't until years later when Dave Wootton (he had made furniture with Peter) found a photo from the 1890s in the Somerset Museum. They had rebuilt the Mill very much as it was back in the black and white picture postcard.

The Spirits of the Mill were very happy that Peter and Fran had brought Pulhams Mill back to life. They would have been even happier if they had managed to get it working as a grain mill again. But they had brought the Mill back to life. As time went on, they were happy that some of the more sensitive customers in the tea rooms could feel their presence.

Anna Miller (1607) would make her presence felt occasionally, but she was never able to find out what had happened to her son after she died. She couldn't rest until she found out if he had lived a full life and if there were any descendants. She had questioned the other spirits. None of them were very friendly; they all had their own agendas. But that is another story.

(VIII)
A CHANGE OF LIFE PLAN

Time went on and they decided to stay at the Mill. What started as a long holiday in the UK ended up as 42 years. Peter flew back to Sydney to sell their business, leaving Fran to look after the Mill. Fran was getting well-known for her artwork. She published a series of books that she illustrated. They opened the craft shop selling hand-made furniture and paintings in the beautiful, historic stone barn that Bertie had used as a whelping pen for his sheepdog puppies. They kept all the features like the king post trusses and the oak shutters. Peter converted the double oak doors into a large double glassed window.

Up until they opened the craft shop, they had been selling wholesale to other outlets. Peter had been taking his furniture and Fran's hand-painted china to craft fairs as far away as Harrogate in Yorkshire. They weren't making a fortune, but it kept the wolf from the door.

(IX)
THE TEA ROOMS, 2000

The Spirits were not very happy that the ancient part of the Mill was to be a tea room. They felt that it was gentrifying their property. They contrived to put a lot of obstacles in the way. They infected the Exmoor planners and the parish council with their opposition. It took two years to get the planners onside. Then the Spirits got the parish to put all sorts of restrictions on how Peter and Fran were allowed to run it.

Not deterred by all this opposition, the plan went ahead. They opened the Riverside Tea Rooms for business in August 2003, having added a commercial kitchen and an extra bedroom and a bathroom and en-suite above. Fran started doing Sunday lunches, which fast became very popular. This brought new customers.

They might have originally opposed the tea rooms, but the Spirits did approve of the quirky people from all over the world who made the effort to come to visit them, some of whom even felt their presence. It broke the boredom of eternal bickering as to who had the right to be at the Mill. Some of the people and things that happened over 20 years really amused them.

(X)
THE CHATTY CHICKEN MAN

It was a bright sunny weekday morning at about 11 a.m., and Grace, the Philippine cook, was in the kitchen preparing the leek and potato soup for lunch. She served Fred, a rough-looking country bloke on his own, who came in for tea and scones. He finished and said that he had no money but could he pay with eggs. Grace said he should go and ask Fran who was in the barn shop, as she was the owner.

Fran told him, 'We have enough eggs, thanks, but maybe the policeman who has just pulled into the car park might want some eggs.'

He said, 'I'll just get some cash from the car.' But he saw the police car and tried to do a runner.

It was fast turning into a farce: very over the top!

A black armed response car with blacked-out windows like something out of a James Bond film, screeched to a halt. Then it was off after Fred. He had run over the fields to take cover. The driver of the response car (not a four-wheel drive) tried to follow him and got stuck. The six armed detectives tried to follow him on foot. They got stuck, too, and lost their shoes in the boggy field. Fred had run around the edges to avoid it. Then a black police helicopter swooped low over the village before landing near Shining Stone (a large outcrop of quartz). After a two-hour chase, eight heavily armed policemen managed to catch him three miles away. It was really overkill!

Fred had stolen a very old Land Rover with a few old, rusty pieces of hedging equipment, 12 eggs and two chickens. He was well known to all the locals and the local bobby. He regularly stole an old Land Rover and other stuff just so he would be arrested and have a night in the police cells and a hot meal. *And this was the reason for calling armed response and a helicopter?*

By the time the whisper got around the village, he had been in possession of three automatic weapons, two axes and a machete.

The response car was really stuck in the boggy field and it took three days and three tractors to retrieve it. In the end, the only vehicle able to pull them all out was a track bulldozer. The local copper had to stay with the Land Rover until it was picked up by a transporter. Fred was arrested and taken to Taunton Gaol.

CHAPTER 14

The Second Auction

PULHAMS MILL, NOVEMBER 2020

The last auction had not worked. As a result, Paul Borrows, trying to regain his losses, had offered to auction Pulhams Mill again. It wasn't the best time of the year. He thought April the 21st would be better – just before the Covid-19 latest lockdown started, as Peter and Fran, the owners were keen to sell. Paul offered to start the ball rolling and auction the Mill before Christmas. This time it was going to be a Zoom auction.

Paul had contacted the BBC as he had previously been the auctioneer on *When the Hammer Falls* (property auctions). The producer, Phil Bingham, was keen to put it on BBC2 live. This was the first live Zoom virtual auction. In the two hours before the auction, the prospective buyers could have a virtual tour, which would continue during the auction. The tour was to go live on BBC2 at 11 a.m.

As the time of the auction approached, ethereal music was emanating from the Mill walls. Paul thought that this was something to do with the TV production, but Phil, the producer, was getting anxious as this was not on his programme.

'I don't know where that's coming from. Never mind, we'll go with it. It suits the building.'

Then, there were appearances on the monitors, shapes that slowly materialised into figures dancing across the virtual cameras, but Paul and the BBC crew couldn't see them for real!

As the start of the live auction on air grew closer, more and more figures appeared on the multiscreen. They seemed to be having a party, all dressed in costumes from history ranging over 1,000 years.

Then the arguments started.

Jerry Winzor (1945), in army No 1's, tried to gather the Spirits together:

'The rightful owner is Francis Pestone, **Frank Westcott's** son. He is 104 and living in France.'

Frank Westcott (1914):
'I was the hero who rescued Colonel Dru from a train in the Pyrenees and left the Mill in the care of Eloise so that my son would have a home.'

Robert Miller (1490):
'Who are you? You didn't even die here. Keep your nose out! I won the Mill at cards for my father, so I have rights.'

Edmund, the Younger (1086):
'The mill was in the lordship of Gytha Harrold's mother. She bequeathed it to my father, Edmund the Elder.'

Anna Miller (1607):
'I have more rights than any of you! My son was disinherited by the Wyndhams.'

Eloise Preston:
'I didn't die here, but my only love, Frank Westcott, was buried here. I was gifted the Mill by the Dru family as they were grateful for his saving Peters Dru's life and we have paperwork to prove it. We want sympatric people to buy the Mill.

If Peter and Fran had not bought the Mill, it would have just fallen down. Peter and Fran had arranged for Johnathon Yodel, a friend who was in touch with the spiritual world as a shaman, to be present at the auction. He was late!

Paul recognised some of the Spirits from the previous auction, but they had been joined by people in WWI and WWII army uniforms as 11 a.m. arrived. Paul hit the gavel to start the auction.

THE AUCTION ROOM

All fell silent, frozen in time. The cameras, lights and monitors blanked for about 30 seconds (half a minute on TV is a lifetime). Phil and David, the director, were panicking. There was a power outage to the equipment; the technical guys were at a loss. Nothing was happening.

This never happened with modern kit.

There was a sigh of relief!

Everything came back to life.

Paul tried to start the auction; the multiscreen monitor showed 20 buyers on Zoom waiting for it to begin.

The Spirits' gathering was appearing behind buyers on the screens, and they were making gestures, rude signs and dancing across in front of them. The buyers weren't aware of this. The whole auction was becoming a farce. The BBC cameras were now picking up these quirkily dressed Spirits fighting with assorted weapons that ranged from medieval swords and bardiches to WWI 303 rifles with bayonets and knives. Even some scallywags spirit lad joined in with a toy machine gun water pistol. (Where did he come from?)

The buyers thought that this was part of the TV entertainment and were laughing and encouraging it.

Johnathon Yodel arrived. He tried to walk in front of the cameras. David, the director, barred his way. 'Can't you see the red light? ON-AIR. Just sit there.'

Johnathon took no notice. He thought he knew how to deal with these wayward Spirits, but they were in such a rage at each other. Although they had all these weapons, they didn't have any effect.

When Robert Miller swung an axe to behead Jerry Winzor, it just took a chunk out of the oak upright and knocked the virtual camera over. 'How did that happen?' Johnathon wondered, as these weapons didn't really exist in the real world. (What is real?) Now he was beginning to doubt his own extensive positive powers as a shaman.

At 11.15 a.m., Paul struck the block with his gavel again. All fell silent again. All went dead again.

Phil said, 'It's the last time I have anything to do with your live auctions; it's a bloody disaster. I'm probably going to get the sack over this. We're off the air now. Go to an in-house ad for that comedy *Ghosts*. My boss will love this because he didn't want to do this in the first place.'

'Can you get this together before we lose our slot?'

'Too late. We've gone to a filler!'

The buyers were still online because they were in the show.

The spirit of Jerry took over the auction. His apparition appeared on all the screens. Paul was at a loss. Then there was a very loud chattering like a giant fan. This deafening sound blanked out everything.

All the BBC monitors and virtual screens fluttered and pixelated, and the auction buyers disappeared. The sound was getting louder and more insistent. A dark shadow moved across the Mill. This was all very real.

Paul, Johnathon Yodel and the production team were looking out of the windows. They could just see through the dust, half of the hedge, branches, leaves, debris of all sorts, and a garden shed door being tossed and broken up by a tornado of wind. They thought that this was the Spirits trying to upset the auction again.

Aerial view of the auction site

There was a shadow of a monster above, materialising into a very tattered-looking but very real beast. The weight of the shadow was bearing down on them. The monster hovered about 10 feet above the roof of Green Oak Barn. It tipped forward to rise above the Mill.

The front rotors were too near the roof of the stone barn. They cut into the roof of the barn and picked up slates, wood, and stone and threw them at the speed of bullets or ancient cannonballs towards the Mill, cutting through the windows frames and sending glass and chips of wood flying in all directions. Broken glass was flying and shredding the curtains and cutting through anything in its path. Paul and the BBC crew were lucky to be sheltered behind the stone portal of the carpet room. Johnathon Yodel was not so lucky. He had run the wrong way onto the road and was caught by a slate as he ran into the open. A part of the rotor sliced through his legs, and a large piece of masonry hit his head.

He was dead before he hit the ground.

Paul and the rest of the crew sustained cuts. There was blood everywhere. They had all run for their lives and escaped through the tea rooms, frantically opening the door into the garden, then across the river away from the Mill.

The rear rotor stopped turning, so the whole fuselage tipped and turned upside down, helpless like an overturned cockroach. The undercarriage resembled its kicking legs. The front rotor stalled and broke up, sending large pieces of very sharp, hardened steel digging into the tarmac and ground at a radius of 30 feet, the body of the helicopter crashed onto the stone mill building, demolishing the roof, crushing the trusses and making a big, impacted groove in the upper floor of the stone walls. Crumbling stones and mortar and wood were falling on Phil's Mercedes parked by the tea room entrance.

The Chinook helicopter came to rest on top of the Mill. The cockpit wasn't crushed. It was totally upside down. It was sticking out over the road. Glass and the frame had been smashed. The pilot and co-pilot were hanging on to their safety belts, and although barely conscious, they appeared to be unhurt. There was a very strong smell of aviation fuel.

For what seemed like hours (probably only half a minute or so), there was a moment of complete silence – the calm after the storm – just the occasional stone falling and the river trickling by. Then the stone wall at the rear of the Mill settled and crumbled under the unaccustomed weight. A window frame, hanging on by a strip of the curtain, dropped to the floor, and the glass smashed.

Then, an eerie quiet, a feeling of foreboding. They could hear the sirens of the rescue vehicles fast approaching (the captain had sent a Mayday that he was about to crash, and an automatic location was transmitted).

Paul and the BBC crew very tentatively came forward to try to help the pilots. At first, they couldn't reach them, but then the captain cut his safety harness and dropped. He had held on to one part of the belt, so he only dropped to about 3 feet above the road. He landed like a ballerina on his feet.

'Freddy, my co-pilot, was hit by a piece of stone. He's unconscious. We need a ladder to get him out,' he shouted.

The sirens from all directions grew louder; they were just in the valley. A police car came from the Dulverton direction and screeched to a halt at Mill Cross. The first responders arrived in the fire and rescue van. Just as the fire engines arrived, there was a sort of popping noise inside the fuselage. Smoke was billowing out through many holes.

The firemen were holding off. Then, the fire chief broke the rules and brought in an aluminium ladder and tackle. They set up a net so that if Freddy fell, he'd be saved from further injury. Brian, the fire chief, mounted the ladder and was just about to lower Freddy down when things started to happen inside the aircraft's body; Brian cut Freddy's safety harness, and he fell into the net.

Just in time. As flames started billowing out, Brian jumped into the net as the fire crew pulled the net and frame clear. Carrying Freddy, they ran as far and as fast as they could across the river bridge.

An explosion in the rear engine ripped apart the fuel tank, throwing a storm of burning fuel raining over the whole scene!

Everyone ran from the wreck. The fire engines on the other side of the river had already started pumping foam to try to dowse the flames and cool everything down. But there were two more explosions. The Chinook was engulfed in flames. More of the top floor of the Mill collapsed, and burning timbers fell on the road, melting and setting light to the tarmac.

Fran, holding on to Peter, was in floods of tears, watching the last 42 years of their work and life going up in flames.

The ambulances and BBC and ITV news teams arrived.

The whole of the valley resembled an American disaster movie set. The flames died down a little. Then there were the odd, small explosions, like shotgun cartridges going off. Slowly everything quietened down.

Everyone seemed to have forgotten poor Johnathon Yodel. It was impossible to get anywhere near his blackened body while the fire was raging. His blood had dried to a dark stain on the road. Eventually, Dave Topps and Barry Gordon (the ambulance attendants) had the unpleasant task of trying to collect his legs, and putting him together, and lifting him to take him away.

THE AUCTION ROOM

There was smoke rising from the remains of the aircraft. It was hardly recognisable as the helicopter that had crashed two hours ago. Ironically, it looked as if the only way to move the carcass from the site would be to use another Chinook to lift it. The road would be shut to traffic until the Fleet Air Arm could move it.

The tarmac had melted. Stone, burned wood, glass, and broken slates littered the road. The fire crew spent most of the two days making sure that the building was secure. The hoses were kept running to cool the whole site so that there were no further outbreaks. They were hoping that it would rain as that would help.

Epilogue

RUIN OF PULHAMS MILL A WEEK LATER

Peter and Fran had been taken to stay in the village by Babs Davis; she had a spare room since her husband had died, and she was glad of the company. All three walked down to Mill Cross. Fran burst into tears again. To see the devastation wrought on forty years of their lives. There were half a dozen vehicles at the crossroads: highway repair and Naval Fleet Air Arm accident recovery trucks. The road was closed, and they were stopped by an officious jobsworth in a dayglow coat, coffee mug in hand.

'Where's your pass? Can't go down there! Health and safety.'

Babs was having none of this, 'Don't you speak to us like that? Don't be ridiculous. This is the owner of the Mill. Fran and Peter have every right. Can't you see they are very upset? They need to go and inspect their property. Let us through at once!'

Babs had made him feel like a naughty child; he morosely stood aside. Hand in hand, Fran and Peter, Babs behind them, walked down to the bridge and sat on the stone wall. They were still in a state of shock. Their whole life was strewn across the road.

As they sat there looking, smoke still gently pluming out of the remains, several apparitions of the Spirits appeared. As usual, they were arguing. This time it was about whose fault this disaster was. And now there was a new Spirit – that of Johnathon Yodel.

'Shut up, you lot! You've done enough harm already; Fran and Peter deserved better.'

'You could have stopped this from happening.'

'But you were too busy arguing about who owns this beautiful ancient building.'

'If you had let the auction continue, the right person could have bought it and given **Pulhams Mill life another thousand years.**'

THE AUTHOR

POWERS IAN MAWBY

As a dyslectic, Ian (Powers) at the age of 80 found his voice. He never even dreamed of writing. As a child he was treated as a 'dunce'. He had fought this disability all his life. This had the result of producing varied and interesting directions of his 6 lives. He was found by David, a son that he didn't know existed, whose story had to be written down (that's another book)! This opened up a Pandora's Box of stories. One of these stories *The Spirits of Pulhams Mill - The Auction Room*, is a Fact/Fictional History of the spirits that inhabited an ancient Doom Day (1086) Mill in Somerset and resisted the Auction sale in 2020.

Ian (Powers) and Pauline his wife bought Pulhams Mill, a romantic ruin, while on holiday from Sydney, Australia in 1978, and spent 40 years building it into a popular destination, Craft Centre, furniture shop, and Tearooms in Brompton Regis, Somerset, England.

Sharing a Lancaster Gate Bayswater flat with 4 other blokes, Ian left 1960s London on a journey of a lifetime on an overland trip on a Magic Bus in 1967, through Europe, Greece, Turkey, Afghanistan, Pakistan, India,

Thailand, Burma, Malesia, and Indonesia, ending up in Sydney, Australia. He met Pauline, an artist illustrator working in a graphic Art Studio, and they started and ran a business for 10 years "*William XX11I*" in the very trendy Paddington & Woollahra at 33 William St, Paddington, Sydney. Here, Ian developed his craft in bespoke Furniture Making and Wood Sculpture, and opened a workshop and showroom at 96 Albion St, Sydney.

THE ILLUSTRATOR

PAULINE ANN CLEMENTS

Born in the Sussex Countryside in 1950, she developed an appreciation and love of the old buildings and countryside around her. Her parents, Rob & Peg, and her sister Carolle immigrated to Sydney, Australia in 1959 where she was trained as an Artist Illustrator. In the early 70s, Ian her husband and she opened their craft shop *"William XXX111"* in Sydney, where, drawing Iron laced Paddington Terraces became her passion. She published her first illustrated book *The Terrace Times Cookbook*, which became a best seller overnight, selling 100,000 copies worldwide in the first year. Subsequently, she illustrated & published three more books, *The Balmain Cookbook*, *The Rocks Cook Book*, and *A Tiny Utopia* in Australia.

On retuning to England, Ian and Pauline bought the ancient (1086) Pulhams Mill on Exmoor. She was then commissioned to supply the over 80 illustrations on gift items of historic buildings in the UK, National Trust, York Minster and internationally in the USA and Ascension Islands. Pauline illustrated and published 5 Devon, Somerset, Cornwall, and Avon books in the acclaimed

Nutshell series and *A Picture of Health - Nearly Vegetarian Cook Book.*

She has hand and individually painted country scenes and animals and flowers on bone china which she is now retailing though her latest venture *"GOLD RUSH----THE MEANING OF LIFE"* at 42 Gold St, Tiverton in Devon, England.

Printed in Poland
by Amazon Fulfillment
Poland Sp. z o.o., Wrocław